Valentine for a Waitress

Rufus Goodwin

Educare Press
Seattle   New York   Berne

FIRST EDITION

Published by Educare Press
2802 NW Market, Suite 308
Seattle, WA 98107

Copyright © 2001 Rufus Goodwin

All rights reserved. No part of this book shall be reproduced, stored in a retrieval system or transmitted by any means, electronic, mechanical, photocopying, recording, or otherwise, without written permission from the publisher.

International Standard Book Number: 0-944638-27-9.
Library of Congress Cataloging Card Number: 2001096548

Printed in United States of America
10 9 8 7 6 5 4 3 2 1

Other works by Rufus Goodwin

Soul Street
North Flame
Souvenirs of a Century
Poems from 42nd Street
Give Us This Day
Poets Novel
Mr. President

Valentine for a Waitress

All characters in this novella are fictional and any resemblance to persons living or dead is coincidental, as is any resemblance to places other than Sicily, or to any establishments.

Forever to Irmele

Part One

Gino's

Rosalie worked at Gino's. Gino's, a family blue-collar and middle-class place, featured poofy booths, wide and ample for a bulky clientele. It was appointed comfortably with a splash of the-night-out for customers who wanted an away-from-home feeling yet it still offered moderate comfiness. The waitresses had to wear black pants and white blouses and neckties, but not coats. Gino's spaciousness was familiar; it could handle family, and either the doctor or the truck driver equally, without discrimination. It was designed for the community.

Gino's customers didn't want fancy dining but they didn't want a truck stop either. Gino's was no barbecue and spare ribs joint, nor a fast food place, but it had to be finger licking good. People had to know what they were getting. It was a gourmand rather than a gourmet place; the portions were more than ample, as ample as many of the customers. The bar dished up drinks at the tables. It was a place to feel good and eat hearty, but not feel pressured in manners or dress. It made for a night out, but nothing over fancy.

Veal parm was the featured dish. Veal parm was Rosalie's favorite. It had that meaty, substantial style, dashed with thick red sauce in big portions. Veal parm suited the stomach and had no unpronounceable French name. The big slop of sauce on the meat was the kind of thing that had visual and stomach appeal to Gino's clientele. It went down with the Chianti. It was a stopper. Gino's was the kind of place where you didn't have to know the specialties or other refinements to eat well - you could just order the veal parm.

Whenever Rosalie couldn't think of something to do or something to say, whenever she wanted to treat me special, to reward me, or to make up for something she would say, 'Let's go to Gino's for a veal parm.'

It was like Sunday, ice cream, or apple pie. She had served it so many times that her mouth watered for it whenever we were out driving with nowhere to go. Veal parm was not her idea of heaven, but of earth.

Besides, she longed to sit in Gino's, on the other side of the booth, and to be served in the place where she had herself served so many shifts. She knew the menu like the back of her hand and it warmed her to go where she had so often served and to sit - to be the one being waited on. Veal parm was the ritual: she had seen so many people's appetite stanched and fed by veal parm that for her it meant a kind of reward. It meant the world was all right. It meant you had enjoyed.

If anything was wrong with her man, if she wanted to put things right, wanted to treat - her man, or herself - there was nothing like veal parm. Veal parm and the Roquefort salad with walnuts. Gino's may not have been fine dining, but it was good eating. Veal parm said it all.

Veal Parm

At Gino's, I dined, for the first time, without telling Rosalie that I was coming, to check out not only the restaurant, but her. The place, as I've said, was ample, with large booths covered in imitation red leather. Partitions and posts and backs separated each booth. There was a bar and a mezzanine, some art on the walls, second generation Italian stuff, classic imitations of nobles eating, and even religious themes.

The ceiling rose fairly high and the kitchen doors swung double, with portholes on either side. The staff wore black pants, white blouses, and neckties.

The hostess seated me at a booth for four, not on Rosalie's station. I saw her, though, at the busboy's stand getting an order straight. She didn't spot me right away.

She looked alert, clean, professional. She moved with swiftness. Rosalie was slight, and, although solid for her size, by no means fat. She stood trim. Shapely. Her black uniform gave her that professional look. The necktie suited her.

When I saw where she was working, I moved to her station, although it was against the rules, and then, when she came out of the kitchen, I went over to her at the busboy stand and greeted her.

She was startled, although she quickly recovered.

"Come to check me out, did you?"

"No," I lied. "I came for the veal parm."

"You should have told me. I can't sit with you. It's not allowed." She gave me a peppery little kiss.

I sat down and thought about her. Rosalie, I realized, didn't have an agenda. Oh, she might want to get married, all right, but she didn't have the usual program of equal rights, entitlement, political correctness, distribution of wealth, dressing like a man, getting back at people, criticizing, backbiting, and malice generally. She had none of that.

Instead of an agenda, she had values. Basics, with a few frills, maybe, in the dressing up and shopping department. But fundamentally it was family, work, pay your debts, marriage, a man, a house and, well, decency. Cleanliness and decency. There was nothing political about her. She was not educated or empowered. She said things straight. She wasn't problematical. She was a scrapper and a fighter, but for basics. She paid her mortgage, kept her credit card down, and bought bargains. If I had to sum it up, I would say she was the basics without malice.

That was what she had of a philosophy. Other than that, she was just full of vinegar. I tried to imagine, if I were eating here for the first time, if I would choose Rosalie for my girl, just by looking at her. I had always been attracted to waitresses.

But they had to have the stuff. It was the action that got to me: they were in constant motion. The ones I liked had that certain swiftness or, maybe, the nerves. Serving kept a body on the go. Maybe it was just basics too: counting, remembering, carrying, clearing, serving.

I liked my conversations with waitresses. I mean, there they were: pretty, cheerful, ready, lively, but all you said was 'please' and 'thank you'.

Maybe it was giving orders that straightened things

out. There was no question what to talk about. No doubt. You didn't have to think about what you said or what they said - it was all in the way it was said. A waitress was all how and not what.

Usually, I liked the aprons too. You don't get to see girls in aprons anymore. And those white shoes. Rosalie's outfit cut it fine too. It was like a uniform. She might have been the usher at a circus, or a theater. She had her little pad and pencil. This was all business and no fooling around. Maybe that is how it should be. I ordered the veal parm.

She kept coming and going, bouncing as she went with the tray in and out the kitchen. I couldn't take my eyes off her. She seemed to me like the starlet in a theater who plays the waitress. It was all like a big play, the extras sitting at the tables, but the waitress catching the eye - like a French comedy.

When she did come back, I don't know if it was the emotion, or my checking her out, or something of her own on her mind, but she just slipped right in front of the booth. The veal parm slid off the tray, and a whole plate of sauce splashed right on my head, slopping down, sloshing on to my shirt. It was hot.

In the booth, I was a pretty mess.

Rosalie for a moment didn't know what to do. Then she smiled her angelic smile and wiped my face with the napkin. I was covered in veal parm and tomato sauce.

"You look like a matador," she said, for no reason at all. "I've never spilled anything. Never even broken a plate. It's all your fault."

She put the veal parm back on the plate and looked at it resolutely.

"I guess you won't be eating this," she said, with a

certain puzzlement. "You should have told me you were coming." She got a towel and mopped me off and cleaned up the table.

"I don't think I'm hungry," I said apologetically.

"Maybe you'd like something else?"

"No. Veal parm was it."

"Well. That's what you got. You're not mad, are you? I mean, it was a mistake," she said.

"No. I'm not mad. Give me the bill."

Rosalie said I didn't have to pay.

I insisted.

Finally, I gave her twenty-five dollars, but she wouldn't take them. So I left them on the table.

"I guess I'll go and have a hamburger," I said.

Somehow she looked awfully glad.

"Call me!" she said. She smiled her angelic smile.

The Trailer

The trailer stood on God's acre with an American flag hanging from beside the door, limply, as if some forgotten war had just ended.

A short driveway led to a plastic shed roof that housed the missing car. There was even a lawn. On the lawn were little rocks from some river making a border, with orange zinnias in bloom. A small bedraggled willow looked like it needed water and its leaves, what there were of them, had already turned yellow. By the trailer door sat a large orange pumpkin that looked as if it were about to burst, but it was brighter and in better shape than the trailer itself. It looked like nobody was at home. It looked as if nobody ever would be at home.

Yet it was somebody's home.

The American dream.

"Somebody lives here," I said.

Rosalie shook her head in disbelief. She wondered why I was stopping here. It wasn't exactly a snowy evening by the woods. There was an old beaten up bike by the stoop, which had a plastic canopy.

All around the beautiful fall foliage glared lovingly in the sun. The landscape was a poem, all russet, gold, orange, yellow, and lavender. Yet there the trailer stood, as if discarded, like an old car wreck in the country.

19

I kept looking at it. What was wrong? Hadn't I ever seen a trailer before, the vestige of a house, a throwaway culture's tin and aluminum answer to the housing of the late twentieth century, with an antenna on top?

It seemed like a long way from nowhere to live here on the countryside, in a place called Somewhere, USA, in a trailer, as if life were following the footsteps of the economy down depression road into a field of forgotten corn, corn that grew America, that fed the cows that produced the beef. Who were these people anyway?

Why, she thought, did I come here?

"Is the cup half full, or half empty?" I said, as if dreaming about living here.

That would be all Rosalie needed: a trailer.

"What cup?" she said.

"The cup of life," I answered, which was just like me. I brought her to the country, the beautiful country of hills, and mountains, and streams, and foliage, and then I held her hand and brought her to a trailer, just standing there, looking at it. And then, because I was a fabulist, I talked about the cup of life. She wondered if she would ever get back to the city.

"There is dream A, and dream B, and dream C. They're all models of the American dream. So what do you think?"

She looked again at the trailer.

"I think it's a dump, that's what," she said.

"A dump?" I said and looked hurt. "These people probably came from Greece or Afghanistan and you know how people live there. Maybe they came from the tenements of Hamburg, or Dresden, or Berlin. Or from behind the Iron Curtain. From Russia. In the old country they dreamed of God's acre and a home and a lawn and some zinnias. Of a freehold in the country of opportunity. The pursuit of happiness. And now they have it. They own it. They even have the flag out."

She knew better, of course. People from Hamburg, or Dresden, or Berlin, from Russia, even from Afghanistan would never live like this. He couldn't fool her. These people were Americans.

Then she realized what I was doing.

I was setting her up. I was planning to move here. I was planning to buy the trailer and live here for ever after. It was my idea of a poem.

"Look at the lantern!" she said brightly.

Indeed, we noticed a brass lantern brightening up the entrance to the trailer. It was polished and shiny. There were glass doors too, patio doors, that had been set into the end of the trailer and that opened on to a small wood patio.

"This is our place," she said mockingly, like a parrot. "We've finally found it. We can come here and live happily for ever after."

I looked at her gladly. She understood.

"Yes," I said, "that's the trailer," as if we were living in a movie and this was the preview of a new feature. The film of our lives. I could see now that she was my kind of girl.

She understood a dream, and that was all that mattered to me, standing here, for a moment, thinking that I could live with her forever and we would never die and we would own it all, no mortgage, able to grow our own vegetables in the back yard. Even the taxes would be low.

"A castle," I said.

For a moment she seemed like the princess I had been looking for, the one who could tell if there was a pea in the bed under the mattress, could spin gold from straw, and could throw a frog against the wall and have it turn into a prince. I would be that prince.

We would even vote for the President of the United States.

One man, one vote - one trailer, one vote.

But it wasn't for sale. She smiled. She had outsmarted me for a moment, let me have my dream, the dream of living in Somewhere, USA, with the zinnias, the foliage, and the American flag. One nation indivisible. Justice and liberty for all. I began to whimper.

"Shall I say the pledge of allegiance right here, now?" I asked her. She was embarrassed.

"No," she said, "the police might see us."

So I saluted. I was saluting a dream. A poem. I was saluting my life with her, our secret nights, our nonsense days, our right to travel, our right to look at a trailer. I was saluting the American flag.

It was all a new love game with me, she realized, and this was my way of flirting with her. I was just offering to take her away from her life as a waitress.

Rosalie was surprised at herself for having gotten anxious for a moment. She thought of where she came from, where she was, and where she was going. The fact was, she thought that I was sort of strange. A trailer? What she liked herself was to go dancing.

Then the Cadillac drove up. Shining black. An Eldorado. Snazzy. Sleek. Spitshined. It reflected the sun, the sky, the leaves, and it turned in front of us into the trailer, just as if it didn't matter what kind of home people had, and came to a stop in front of the American flag and in front of the pumpkin. She remembered it would soon be Halloween. The day of all souls, the day of the dead.

The Cadillac stopped.

Until then Rosalie hadn't realized that all this was not a dream, not a poem, not a joke, but deadly serious, and she quickly took me by the hand and started down the long road that led from Somewhere, USA, to Somewhere Else, USA, another place around the corner, on the road of life.

She could feel her feet on the asphalt.

It was a long way to wherever we were going, and I seemed to be looking back to the trailer. We had so much love together it was almost scary.

Then she said in a quiet voice filled with the desperation of her life and all her dreams, "I will never, never, never, *ever* live in a trailer."

The Apron

Waitresses serve tables all over America. From counters and coffee tops, to cafeterias and diners, to bookshops and drugstores, to restaurants and nightclubs. Eateries in hotels and airports have them. Even Italian restaurants in America feature waitresses. Girls come from all walks of life to serve and waitress; some even have other jobs but can use the money.

The apron used to be the sign of a waitress. Many of them now wear pants like men, and you can see them lifting their arms to pour coffee, pull spouts, lift trays. Bar girls too belong to the profession, the ones making the drinks and serving cocktails. Black used to be the color of choice, short black skirts or black pants. A waitress has a kind of uniform - no frills to get in the way of the food, hair usually short, or pulled tightly back, sometimes a headband or comb or ribbon or restraint.

"On the floor I'm zooming around," said Rosalie, "tables all over the place. Today it went better, but the kitchen was sloppyish. They had us making our own salads. And all that sour cream, tartar sauce, thousands of appetizers and fried food. It was tough hours. But you know I get good ones, the tips. You gotta get those trays out at the buzzer. The expeditor already has the dishes on the tray. Grab those trays! But they like me so good I'm going to be able to call my own hours, you know what I'm saying? I usually carry on the right, but now they got those doors on the left. The door slammed on my tray and I almost lost it because I'm pushing from the right, you know what I'm saying?" Waitressing is an attitude.

Of course, many waitresses are brief and matter of fact, particularly the ones without much experience - the part-time job girls, not the professionals.

The ones who really make it their living are often cheerful and attentive, waiting on the customer literally, like it says - to wait. The customer takes a long time to think of what to have and reads the menu. Waitresses are patient. They make small talk.

They say, "Nice day today," and, "Have a good one." They watch how people are getting on. They watch for the empty cup of coffee. The time to clear. But it's not just the small things. It's the action. The myth. The way of being.

Doctors, lawyers, teachers have their niche in our society, and so do policemen, truck drivers and cabbies. All these stalwarts of our world make the culture run. They are like signposts of our civilization. The types of the cast. We recognize our way of life by them, our everyday humanity.

But waitresses are even more so. And more than that, they are always someone to talk to, to have a few words with, just "Good morning," maybe, or, "Would you like another cup of coffee?" They are the leftover mothers of culture. The stand-ins for the maternity we have all left behind. They are role models for the common touch, the small courtesy, the little kindness that we squeeze out of everyday life.

They are girls too. And women. They represent their kind, a sort of gender presence in the plates, forks and spoons of life, the face, the breasts, the buttocks that men look at over the cup of coffee of life.

The hairdo. But always they know their place - it is okay to be fresh with a waitress, but only up to a point; and the waitress can be friendly, but only up to a point. It's the profession. Custom controls it - friendliness, but not too much fraternizing. Waitresses always have a certain kind of discipline, like nurses: as well as the friendly touch, they know how to keep the customers at a certain distance.

Rosalie, the waitress, in fact, was one of the American icons.

Like the cowboy, the gangster, the movie star, the trial lawyer, the tycoon, the millionaire, the farmer, the bumpkin, the railroad man, the construction worker, the shopkeeper - the waitress is *on*, of the basic types, as if the characters of the culture in our lives were stock players.

"Rosalie," I said to her, "you know what? You're a stock type."

"A stock what?"

"Type."

"You have lots to learn," she said.

Yet millions of different types of women and girls are waitresses, like typists, secretaries, nurses. Only waitresses keep moving. They don't sit. They are in constant action. Back and forth, from the inner sanctum, the kitchen, with their pencils and order pads. And their shoes are always business like, Oxfords, it used to be, or now walking shoes, or sneakers, or Nikes, because they are on their feet for hours.

"You could work at the hospital," I told her. "You could be a medical assistant."

"And pass up the tips?" she said. That's when I realized it was a lottery for her. Some days fat, some days thin. She liked the action.

Waitress glamour is low-keyed too; they aren't in high heels and a lot of makeup. Neat, trim, tidy, ready to wear. Rosalie's was a practical profession. Service, and food, and cleanup. All that sidework. Always a new table to dress up. People come and go, the waitress stays.

Another turnover comes in. People think they are there forever once they sit down with an appetite to eat, that they are the only ones in the world to have ever sat here - but Rosalie has seen them all. It's just another table to turn.

It gives a certain view on life, was what I learned from Rosalie; you don't tend to get so stuck after that, you don't hang up on small things.

"Some of us are practical," she kept telling me. When Rosalie was away, too, at work, there was like a telephone in my heart for her - as if she were there. I missed my waitress, and would plan something special for her. That was my way of missing her, by thinking what I would do for her when I saw her next.

Too, the money she made, became my Dow Jones index; I would wait for the figure every night, like a market. I would look at my watch and realize that she had to be at work in twenty minutes. Or that she was a half hour from being back.

At night I began to count the tables she would turn. I began to get hungry when she went to work. All I wanted to do was get down to Gino's and order the veal parm. But now, when she was working, Gino's was off limits.

Rosalie Talk

Rosalie loved diminutives. Everything was little and sometimes she put an ending, like -ly, or -*ino*, at the end of a word to make it smaller. Sometimes it was as if she spoke another language, not American.

Take love. It was always *lovely*. She would not say, "You are my love." She would say, "You are my lovely."

"I am your womanly," for example, was the way she spoke. "You are my manly."

"Would you like a sandwichly?"

A small dog was a dogly.

A candy was a sweetly.

"Do you have a little lovely for your womanly?"

"Would you like a little supperly?"

You took a naply. You went to sleeply.

All these diminutives were endearments. Rosalie wrapped the world with her soul. Her language made things smaller, more intimate, dearer.

"Are you my dearly?"

"Yesly."

"Goodly. Don't you ever forget that you are my manly."

It wasn't soft or sentimental. She was crisp, alert, and rough-mouthed too.

And orders! She could certainly give orders. She could even bark. "All right, now. Now give me my kissly! Immediately! Kissly! Kissly! Kissly!"

A Body

The shop window was like a wonder glass and, until Rosalie, I had always wanted a mannequin like in the store fronts, on whom the clothes looked so terrific, and who held the same pose forever, dreaming glass-eyed into the glamour of the future as if a woman were a perfect sculpture in a mirror.

Rosalie, instead, was real.

But we were standing one day in front of Bergdorf Goodman and the perfect dress was in the window like a painting. It was a neat, tailored suit in herringbone, gray and white, a size four, and it looked like Rosalie's body. So we went in.

The Fifth Avenue matrons and Jewish princesses and Park Avenue molls and yuppies from all over were parading around looking at multi-thousand dollar outfits and dresses, stepping on people as usual as they wafted up and down the escalators. Rosalie had never been there.

She began looking at items on hangers in alcoves and surrounded by mirrors, but I said, "I want the outfit from the window, accessories and all. Just as it is on the mannequin. I've never had a girl dressed like that and there's something about the glamour in the window that you can't recreate. It's a dream. You buy a dream. I don't care about the clothes. I want the dream. I want you walking out of here like a window, a reflection in glass. What do you say?"

"A mannequin? A little kinky, I'd say. I can get this all at Lucky Lady for a few bucks," she sniffed.

"But not the dream. You buy the dream once in a lifetime. You walk out of here with it on."

She looked dubious.

Then she tried an evening dress on. The saleslady was a working lady in her fifties, motley and matronly, with an ill-fitting black dress over her drooping body. Rosalie treated her like dirt. It was get this and get that. No, this isn't cut right, no this doesn't fit. No this isn't the right size and this isn't the right fit.

The waist is too large, the back sags, the butt isn't cut right. There wasn't a thing that wasn't wrong with everything in Bergdorf Goodman's for Rosalie. You would have thought it was the Aga Khan's wife, the Queen of Bahrain who was buying.

"Rosalie!" I kept whispering to her.

Finally, she told the saleslady nothing was right. She wasn't even sorry. She put her street clothes back on and led me out of the store, between the furred ladies and the jewelry counters, with the rich bitches parading their cosmetic faces and flashing their purses and cards with expensive false teeth and facelifts, out for a shopping spree, a little ten thousand dollar bauble to brighten up the morning.

"At least," Rosalie scoffed, as we revolved around the front door out on to the street, "At least I have a body."

She breathed a sigh of relief.

We passed the mannequin again and she said, "The lady was trying to hang all the clothes on me. These women think they're going to get a magic body. Why should I get something ugly on my body? I have nothing to hide!"

The Foxtrot

Because of Rosalie, I even learned to dance again. This time it was not just twirling around and hopping, but the emotion; Rosalie had the motion. 'I could have danced all night' became not just a song but a new way of looking at life.

Rosalie, even in airports and the restaurant, in the bedroom or on the street, was always doing pirouettes. She literally bounced with dance. Like the breeze blows a feather, music made Rosalie move.

She was a ballroom dancer. This meant dressing and getting pretty. Dancing was going somewhere. Putting on the glitz, powder and rouge.

Rosalie couldn't pass a mirror anywhere without taking a peek into it - and dancing was the same. It was a place in which she saw herself. An image she had.

She looked in shop windows with an eye to how she would look out there on the dance floor. Her mind worked like a movie in which she saw herself dancing.

At first, I was stiff with the years, awkward, clumsy, and slow. I moved like a plank. Besides, I had never really had the steps. I didn't know the routines the way they were supposed to go. But she took me to Musel's, out in the suburbs, a Quonset-type barn at the crossroads, with its sign up on the strip and a few lights. It was like a suburban Wonderland.

All the crowd was older and the musicians looked like they had been playing since the forties and fifties.

The lighting was like in old late night movies, with a shiny wood floor and mirrors. There were decorated columns and lounge lizards hanging around. A glittery bar served the drinks and there was cake and coffee after the fourth set.

The older ones all had jackets and neckties and cocktail dresses on, and the women were made up with rouge. There was a bizarre feeling to the sight, as if old-timers were out for romance way past their bedtime.

It made no difference to me. I was glad to see a crowd that hadn't lost the art. Everything was subdued. People chatted quietly and couples moved flowingly around the dance floor in the night. It seemed like women and men here belonged together. There was something social about the dance.

I was leery to dance again, especially as Rosalie was so practiced and held her head up so high, didn't smile, lifting her arm and hand coolly to the correct position with a professional touch.

Suddenly, one, one two, we were flowing around the dance floor in unison, my leg passing neatly between hers, left on right, the footwork falling into place like an old puzzle.

Things began to light up. I could feel her twist and turn and break, and I began to lengthen my stride, to dip, to flash my head to left and right, to signal the turns, the faces, the breaks, the walks. It was like finding a new self.

When Rosalie danced she wore a smile like an angel, as if she were walking in a mirror, on eggshells, as sweet as cake. It got to me and I climbed out of time into the music and motion as if a dream were unrolling on the screen.

She and I seemed made for each other and fit like

tongue and groove in the tucks and turns, whether it was social dancing, waltz, foxtrot, two-step, quickstep, or the Latin beats, rumba, mambo, meringue, cha-cha, samba.

Slowly we began to show off and dip and turn, brushing up our movements into gestures and shows, forgetting the old crowd. Rosalie would smile her smile and whisper, "We look good." She was on show, a performer, and it made it seem even more fun, as if at a competition, as if the audience were seeing in us new love, like a movie where the man peers from the subway, sees the dance shop and the girl at the window, gets off on the spur of the moment from the train and goes for a lesson in the dance hall, and it starts the affair of his life and he dreams of a waltz with his beautiful instructress.

"You're going to dance the rest of your life," the bartender told me with a touch of envious sarcasm, as if my story would be one of the shoes that made me dance forever until I dropped.

The old swing and jive and the mambo rhythms went to my heart and I seemed to fit better into my body. Like Rosalie after that, whenever I heard the inaudible music on the street, I would begin dancing on the train platform, in marble foyers, wherever there was a little space and surface to move on. A bare patch of glistening floor.

When Rosalie and I came together, moving toward each other, we would look at each other from a few paces off, our hands would fling up and out, our fingers would open, and we would foxtrot into each others' arms.

We began dancing in her kitchen while she was cooking or I was doing the dishes. That professional gaze of hers would come over her face like a study and she would move into the flows and twirls.

Only she complained that I didn't lead, I didn't signal the moves right to her. She had to guess.

"Of course, I know how to dance better than you," she said, "but still, I can't always be expected to guess where you're going."

I told her she was secretly jealous, because, although I didn't have the steps, I had the Latin tempo and I could fake and cover the time.

"You don't have the Latin movement from the waist down," I told her, "you move your chest and shoulders, and bend. You sway. That's not the way it is. The head has to stay just so, entirely still, and the shoulders too. Only the hips wriggle, and the ankles." This was my only way at getting back at her for being a better dancer.

But what she was really working on was the waltz - the bridal waltz.

In her mind, she saw us two out there, her in the white gown, my arm around her waist, her leaning back, the crowd watching, the lights whirring, the film rolling, that slight smile of ecstasy on her slightly parted lips, and the wedding march in the background. They had taught it to her since childhood.

The wedding bells pealed.

That was when to achieve social stardom, security, and fight off loneliness and escape destitution - she was in white, yes, safe at last, and dancing her way to the altar.

No Pennies, Please!

Rosalie, at close quarters, was a pest. She just couldn't leave you alone.

Something was always wrong. I never remember a moment with Rosalie when I didn't have a spot on my clothes. She was obsessive about spots. It had all the force of her early training, as if spots were a metaphor for all that was evil in life.

She must have lived in fear of spots as a child. A spot for her was like her worst enemy. Rich people can afford to be dirty - but not poor people. Whenever we came together the first thing she went over was the clothes to make sure there were no spots. If there was a spot, I had to change. Immediately. Wrinkles too were bad. And hair. She always checked my hair.

"It's going every which way," she would say, and if it was too smooth, she would fluff it up.

Without spots or wrinkles. There was something Biblical about it. That was the way the Bride of Christ was supposed to be in the Bible - the Church.

Yes, Rosalie, for me, meant a complete change in wardrobe. It wasn't your secret assets, your inner self, that counted with Rosalie; it was the upfront appearance.

"What you see is what you get," she said, and she knew it from the job market. First appearances were what counted; they only looked at the resume afterwards.

She might be working poor, but she could afford a full-length mirror. Reflection meant for her not reviewing yourself with your mind, but looking at yourself in the glass. It was part of survival. Rosalie, except for on the job punching the menus into the kitchen, was not in the computer age. She didn't sit at a desk. She didn't have the analytic tools. She wasn't online, except to the kitchen. She wasn't a cyberspace punk with a flat face, a monitor face. She didn't have executive abilities.

She didn't have an educated, in quotes, attitude. She wasn't a college waitress. She was a professional.

Rosalie had the blue collar attitude. A worker's attitude. She knew a job. She knew how to count. She knew honesty. She knew hard work. She knew service.

It was a people thing with her. Solidarity and service. Support and mutuality. Not a question of perks, privileges, and extra pay. But she had pride. She was a woman in her pride. And she knew that part of her value was her appearance.

She wasn't scruffy like the college waitresses. Pride was a possession. Her father had been an auto worker. He produced cars. Rosalie was in service. She produced service.

"What did you make today?" I asked her.

"Good money," she said, laconically.

Not street money, but good money; not market money, nor finance money; not bank money, nor profits - good money. She didn't pull it out of a portfolio. She didn't get it in an envelope under the table. It wasn't interest. It came the honest way. And it made her feel good, every penny, every dollar.

But waitresses didn't like it when people left their pennies in with the tips. That was an insult. It was below

Rosalie. It wasn't professional. She wasn't penny wise and pound foolish, like the Yankees and Wasps out there; she was for dollars and cents - it spelled sense.

When I saw Rosalie at work, I couldn't help seeing all the other millions of American at work, serving, cleaning, scurrying to the kitchen. These were the phalanx of waitresses that fed the hungry. This was where the American manners were. This was eating out. It used to be aprons and bonnets, now it was just good will and a cup of coffee.

But Rosalie was the best. She didn't just serve, she serviced you. From the smile to the chitchat to the coffee to the tip. This was a people profession. It was their night out. And Rosalie was giving them a little something extra for their money.

Oh, she got the orders right, kept the tab, moved the table, turned over the station. That wasn't it. She might have been their personal maid. That was more like it. For a half hour she gave them the impression they had a personal maid that waited on them, fulfilled their every wish.

And she was always neat and made up for the trick. Her crest of hair was in place, sprayed to stiffen it, neat and tidy, with her black pants and white blouse and apron. The way she did it, it was as if she had gloves on.

Whoops! And the heavy tray of dirty dishes and plates was gone. Whoops! And it was all there - cocktail, iced water, salad, entree. She was a little whiz zooming from kitchen to table and back, her little head filled with veal parmigiana, chef's salad, and the drinks.

Yes, it was no pennies, please, for Rosalie.

The Manicure

Rosalie, despite her dainty hands, had never ever had a manicure. No, not in all her life. So I decided to splurge and to book her at the Coco International with Annie for her birthday and get her nails done. She had pretty nails.

But they were worn and tattered with waitressing. Besides, she had to keep them short for work. Her hands, otherwise, were smooth, with well-articulated fingers. She had the prettiest thumb in the world.

I went too with her. They said it was the first time a woman there had ever been accompanied to her manicure by her man. I sat beside her and held her other hand while Annie worked.

Rosalie's thumb was narrow at the base, then knuckled out charmingly at the middle, like a woman's waist, and tapered slightly and athletically toward the tip. The cuticles were layered back and strong. Her thumbnail was slightly pointed. It was a shaped hand. A sculptor had worked on it. It looked like a thumb that could dance.

There was no color or old polish to take off the nails. She had never painted them red. All she ever did was file them. With the trays, they chipped.

Annie was perfectly glad to see Rosalie. It gave them a certain rapport to know that Rosalie had never done her nails before. But I was in the way; Annie didn't care much for an extra man. So I went over nonchalantly to a free seat in the beauty shop where I wouldn't be in their way and began to look at the other cosmeticians and hairdressers at Coco, a snappy crew. Occasionally, I would ask Rosalie how she was doing. It was here, in Coco's, that I first realized how great a movie star Rosalie would have been. Not a glamour beauty, but she was photogenic.

She had the tight structure and smart skin of a Greta Garbo, the pulled back features of Ingrid Bergman, in a word, the European look. Her face was worked through. There was no pudge, no baby smile, no upturned nose.

It was a crooked little face but full of impishness. She had all the mobility and expressiveness of Julietta Masina, Fellini's wife, the star of those existential Italian comedies of life. It was a starlet's face, a comedienne.

It was in motion, but not all the time. In repose, she had a sort of athletic glamour. It was a German face, a Swedish face, a Danish face.

The crop of blonde hair peaked over the widow's crest and Rosalie even set her peak with fixative. Around the sides, it was cropped and layered back. It had that short, urchin, gamin look that the French wear. In fact, she looked like a blonde Colette. But she didn't smoke.

It was her takes. They would bring the house down. Not like a clown's gumminess, because Rosalie was too athletic for that. Her face in miniature was muscular. Her expression, when not in repose, and when not caught in her ecstatic smile, was constantly on the move doing gymnastics. Yet it all had a stamp of her own. It wasn't a wisecracking, joker's face, and she didn't mug - but she was just constantly startled, surprised, mocking, conniving, conspiratorial, mischievous.

"So how does it feel?" I asked her.

She made a face.

"I like the silver," she said, "or the mother of pearl. What do you think?"

Rosalie was terrible about getting herself up.

She would think about it for days. She planned getting dressed like people plan a party meal. And she always wanted to know what I thought. She wanted me to decide.

"Should I wear the gold, the lame, or the black top with the silk pants?" she would ask.

To me, how Rosalie dressed was part of the surprise. But getting to know her better, I thought I would have to dress her. I wanted no part of it, no decision making. I wanted to be pleasantly startled. I wanted her to write the menu.

She always looked good. That wasn't the problem. The problem was that she wanted to co-opt me in the process. She wanted me to involve myself as much in what she would wear, buy, and put on as she herself did.

Sometimes it was all she talked about. She would get ready and plan dressing for an occasion as much as six months ahead of time; I was supposed to know everything in her closet as well as she.

"It's fine, Rosalie," I would say.

"Fine? Just fine?"

Then she would pout.

"I ask my manly what I should wear and then put all this time into making myself pretty for my manly, and he says, 'It's fine'."

Girls having manicures look like pet dogs, with their paws on the counter, and the manicurist bent over painting their nails. It might have been a poodle shop. But Rosalie was no poodle. She was no doll nor rich Missus nor kept lady nor mistress nor cosmetic junky nor model nor fashion hanger - she was a grit and gristle waitress.

Her first manicure was a big success too; because she had so often served, she loved being served. There was no complex in her about patronizing or being patronized. She was just like a girl in a movie having her first manicure and getting all princessed up for an evening out with her man.

"You'll get spoiled," I told her.

"Never," she said, looking at her new fingernails and blowing on them. She waved them in the air. "I'm all ready to dance," she said. "Are you ready to take me out?"

Annie had been a little put out. She was used to working on ladies. It galled her slightly to work on Rosalie. After all, Rosalie was just a working girl.

Working the Dream

"I don't dream the American dream," Rosalie said, "I work the American dream."

She was just off from her station, the second turn of the day, slinging pizza and waiting on thirty-five parties.

On some days, she just went into the kitchen and bit her lips. Of course, other people sometimes left as much as fifty dollars in tips.

Often, because she was the quickest, they gave her the mezzanine; this was four steps up to the tables every time she carried a tray or took an order, and four steps down. She had a bone bruise on the ball of her foot, between the big and second toes.

Rosalie was a size four. One hundred and twenty pounds. That way you found the best bargains, because the fashion dresses that came down to discount couldn't often find the smaller sizes. She spent as little as twenty dollars on dresses sometimes.

She was a blonde still. Of course, it was silver underneath, but gold was her color. Her hair was short with a crest in the front over the brow; her skin was gold too, and she wore browns and yellows. Her eyes were a mixture of gray, green, and blue, like a hazy sky. Her face was drawn and as if she had just run a marathon; it had the intelligence of life written in it and alacrity.

"Some of us," she liked to say, "have to work."

When she ran, it was up on the balls of her feet, her shoulders slightly raised, her arms pumping close to her chest, and she glided or floated forward, not down on the heels of her feet - her motion was onward. It wasn't choppy, but like a well-oiled little piston churning onwards. Her legs and thighs were shaped, lean, and muscular. They weren't thin though. It was her center of gravity, just below the hips, although she was upright and straight. Her face looked like it had been in training. It was not a soft, relaxed face. Nor, when at rest, did it show traces of a smile. It was a serious face. It bore the brunt of life.

But her smile was like a soft breeze. It still had the child of life in it, delighted with some impulse. Her face became sweet, as if never touched by pain, or taken by some wonderful, soft reward.

It was a smile of innocence. Of something simple, something good. There was no revenge, no self-consciousness, no superiority, no selfishness in it. It lit up life.

In fact, whether it was the running, or the waitressing, the heavy trays, the back and forth, there was light in her. She almost shone. It was as if she were a battery that had just been charged.

The Parrots

"I'm just a regular girl," said Rosalie when I tried to explain to her what a fabulist is.

"Look, you want to know what I do for a living," I said. "So I'm trying to tell you what a fabulist is. A fabulist lives a fable. Life is not just your everyday TV show or dishwashing or scrubbing the floor. It's not nine to five and a checkout counter where the laser reads the label. It's not a computer where the mouse clicks open a window and a spread sheet. Life is a story. It's an imagination we make up. It's like living a film that we are shooting. It's a poem that is happening. It's an idea. An idea that is happening. We are pencils in the hand of God. It's not just a stop sign, a traffic light, and a parking meter. It's the eye of God seeing something. An angel..."

"The kisses. I want the kisses," she said, offering her cheek. "I want my man. I want breakfast with my man."

She thought about it again.

"I want to be a family."

So I told her about the parrots.

Parrots live in cages, in couples. There is a girl parrot and a boy parrot. To pass the time, they pick on each other. The way they pick on each other is to take feathers from each other, pecking out the feathers with their bills.

"The strongest parrot wins. They keep pecking each

other out of love until all the feathers are gone. When a parrot has no feathers it dies. Whichever parrot picks all the feathers first lives longest."

To show her what I meant, I put my thumb and forefinger together, leaned over, and plucked an imaginary feather from her arm with a jolt.

"Ouch!" she said. "What did you hit me for?"

"I took a feather. That's what parrots do."

"Give me a break," she said. "Why can't I have a normal boyfriend?"

"You wanted to know what a fabulist is," I told her.

"Well, be whatever it is some other time," she said.

What she really wanted was the wedding. That was her true make-believe. To hell with fabulists and parrots, but now, if you were walking down the aisle, that was real, and for Rosalie anyplace or everyplace was the right place to practice saying "I do." Until then she would just knit.

Oh, she believed in sex all right. That was no problem. It didn't take a wedding to be physical, even with a fabulist.

"A fabulist?" she said. "Why don't you just do it?"

Well, I tried. Rosalie was warm and wonderful, a regular little acrobat, but because she had never had a father, because the first man in her life had marched off to the Eastern Front and never come back, she was unable to have a peak.

All her peaks were plateaus in expectation of some great climax, some great return, that life had taken away from her and she always dreamed of - but the moment never came.

Rosalie needed more, not less, than the next woman and it was as if she was still a girl who had never become the final woman of her life, and she had more hope, more energy, more wishes, and more need for love than ever.

This, far from making her undesirable, made her more

vibrant, more ready, more longing. Life was always ahead of Rosalie. A moment never died without hope. Since she had never quite got there she was always setting out.

She met insult and injury and disillusion with a small grateful smile for what she was to become, for what was to become of her. Nothing in her life had been spoiled by success and surfeit.

Life was yet to come. Her smile was expectation. Maybe her father one of these days would come home. It was the pixie in her.

Yet her eyes were wise.

The Furnished Room

Make no mistake, this story is a homage to her. After all, a waitress makes $2.25 an hour, relying on gratuities and tips, the goodwill of the public.

My Rosalie, in fact, can make $170 on a good night, but that's for eight hours on the job, taking orders, carrying trays, running up and down steps to the booths on the mezzanine.

"Rich bitch," her friend calls her now that she has met a crazy millionaire, a fabulist, but no one knows I'm spending twice as much as I bring in. She wants to know where I make my money, and how - so I say: in the gutter. Picking up pennies. After all, this is a free market, isn't it?

It's not right to make fun of the working person either; the ethic of this country is based on hard work, too, from the days of the Pilgrims and the Calvinists, but you used to get Sunday off before the country decided God was politically incorrect, or, even, illegal. Rosalie worked on Sundays. No extra pay either.

As she said, "One of us has to work."

It wasn't originally her country even. America never belonged to anybody like that, except the Indians, and they came from somewhere too. But Rosalie made it her own; she had been here for years.

Her house was almost paid off too. It was a gray ranch

house in a tract with two bedrooms upstairs and a day room downstairs, one garage, and a deck out back.

I won't even tell you where it was, but it was Somewhere - in Somewhere, USA, blue collar style, a thriving town, in fact, which you wouldn't find anywhere else in the world.

Home, that's what it was, for all those who live there - not like New York, Paris, London, Rome, Calcutta: places in the minds of people everywhere - but just plain living, out there off the Interstates and the East West routes, a regional Somewhere that people are born into and end up in without really knowing why or often what for.

It wasn't a place on the way to anywhere else or anything else. It was just there. Sort of homey, homely, and cozy, and, of course, cheaper.

The trim board was rotting but I suppose it was better than the tenement housing she grew up in, although at least there she had a balcony, and it's not poverty she remembers, but the balcony. Here, they call it a back yard.

Rosalie, mind you, is one plucky girl. Scrappy. Hard scrabble. Some might say scrawny, a scrawny woman, but I don't think so because I dance with her and she moves like music, like a field of grain, in the wind, and has little muscles from slinging pizza and trays, cute little muscles, as she says, and she runs, yes, in the marathons, and those legs are anchored to earth with an acrobat's aplomb and the thighs as shapely as a twenty-six mile run, and she has that blunt little crooked nose and gray green eyes and a smile all her own that is as gay as a star falling out of heaven and grinning with pretty, lovely, secret joy that makes one want to film her as a lady clown in a cabaret act all her own.

She cuts her hair short, gamin-like, with wisps around her neck and a peak in front over her brow that she blops up with spray and stiffens, so that she looks like one of those front page Teutonic blondes, the lithesome, petite kind, not the Wagnerian ones, from the teen hair shops of Cologne, or Dusseldorf, or Hamburg, the one hundred and twenty pound models, size four, in *Brigitte* magazine or *Elle*.

In fact, a long time after meeting her on the airplane, I asked her who she thought she was, and she said, without batting an eye, "I'm your golden girl."

That was after I took her to New York.

We were walking up Fifth Avenue to 57th Street, where she had never been, where General Motors has its building and Trump has his tower, and we passed Cartier's, the jeweler's.

My first wife got a platinum band out of me, about $150 worth, and my second wife actually had to give me the ring, but in Cartier's window was a stunning stone, a Canary diamond, square, sunburst, the size of a goldfinch egg, and my girl had told me yellow was her color, so I said to her, "Look!" and we went in. I just thought it was a lark, like going to a museum of rare monkeys, taking a waitress, worth $2.25 an hour, into Cartier's and not caring the devil about any of it. But she was reading my mind. Even my nephew, who is still young but already married, said to me, "Not even I am that dumb."

Cartier's is like an art gallery with exhibits carefully arranged in peekaboo windows where each exquisite jewel is displayed in a volcanic setting and all the staff are homosexuals, mostly, who looked me over airily and said, "There are some small rings in the back of the store."

My golden girl had never been any place like this and her eyes were gleaming, not with greed, but with love - I don't know where it comes from, because I'm not much, just a fabulist, a piece of used goods and cast off who scarcely deserves the clothes on my back, but she treats me like some kind of poet and her eyes brim with life as if I had just ridden in on a white horse with a million dollars.

Our stone, the one in the window, turned out to be a 16-carat canary from Zaire, dug up by a few of those glistening blacks who used to thrive in the Congo, and now selling for a cool $600,000 on upper Fifth Avenue.

Well, I took her out on the street again, pretty pleased with myself, since I had never been in Cartier's either, but she said, "Show me the stone again."

We stood in front of it holding hands. I just love to hold her hand. It's as if I would never die and had never been alone in my life, and somebody just gave me a free lunch.

I can't get enough of it. When I don't know what to say next I just kiss her hand. She's like the girl in *The Red Shoes* that would dance herself to death if the music lasted, but she looked at our ring and said, "How much is it?"

"Six hundred thousand dollars," I answered.

"I tell you what," she answered. "I'll give you a discount. How about a little one for six hundred dollars?"

It was then I knew how mixed up she was. It wasn't Cartier's, it wasn't the canary diamond, it wasn't us she was thinking about - it was, well, marriage. Yes I was that dumb.

In fact, I still didn't get it. A piece of nothing, like myself, what would she ever want me for? That was about all I was thinking. Certainly not for marriage. But marriage is for a woman: it doesn't matter who.

Our stone. Of course, I had to think fast, so I said, "Well, the truth is I can't afford marriage. But if you're thinking of a ring, I'd hold out for $600,000. You're worth it. Don't go for a penny less." And I dragged her away.

But at the next red stop light, she said, "Just remember, the color is yellow."

Well, I was thinking of her house, its almost being paid off, and the taxes and the upkeep and all, and then of my apartment, which is not right for her, just a studio, and of my new car, and of driving back and forth to see each other, and of her slinging all that pizza and waiting on all those tables for $2.25 an hour, without tips, and I can say it galled me. Love just seems to go to taxes and mortgages and payments; it isn't right. That's what it means to be a crazy millionaire and a fabulist.

If she could rent the house she could bring in $900 a month, and probably clear about seven hundred of it, which gave me a brilliant idea as we reached Park Plaza and the horse and buggies that travel around the park with the couples in them sitting and holding hands.

She looked at me expectantly, as the horses stomped their feet, and I thought this was the perfect moment. Her eyes were so bright and her smile haunted me like some lovely ghost that I wanted to look at forever and never let go.

"You know what?" I said.

Her lips were parted.

"What?" she said.

Looking at her I knew one thing for sure. She wasn't interested in me just for the money. The money, of course, helped. It didn't hurt. I'm not saying that. It was something else.

Not another girl in the world could have helped in her place of thinking about the money first.

It seems like money can solve everything. But it doesn't.

It's love. Love just solves your problem and kills the pain. It sounds banal, but it's true. Looking at her I just wanted to melt. Even the $600,000 ring seemed like a real possibility. It was that real.

"I think I know how to solve your problem," I said.

"What?"

Years in America, all that history, and all that waitressing, yet she was still fresh, eager, and young, as if she just came in on the boat.

She said it again: "What? Tell me!"

"Well," I said. "You know? You could rent the house and live in a furnished room."

The Angel

"It's fun to write checks and pay bills if you have the money," Rosalie used to say, and it made me think of the millions of people who have the money and for whom it is no fun.

I guess it's all in the having and not having.

If you have not, it's fun to have - but it doesn't work the other way round.

"They shut me down at ten o'clock," Rosalie complained, and she was also worried about Valentine's Day. "You get all the deuces," she said. "It's the bigger parties that tip well. Couples always think they can get away for ten per cent."

The other thing that surprised me about Rosalie was that her angel had a name. I guess I didn't even expect her to have an angel. But it was no nameless angel, no anonymous cherubim, although it didn't have a very active metaphysical life, as far as I could tell. But it had a name.

"Mine is a working angel," Rosalie said. "She's got a name. She's not dressed fancy or anything, and I don't even know if she has wings. She has an apron on, and blue overalls."

She told me the angel's name, but I won't repeat it. To me it seemed too holy.

Once, we were in a Christmas shop, and it was snowing.

Beside all the tinsel decorations and ornaments there were angels. One of them was a ragamuffin with a sooty black top hat, rag pants, a white beard, and pointed eyes and a broom.

"That's my angel," I told Rosalie.

It was a homeless angel. She looked at it musingly, wondering what made me pick such a one, then asked, "What's its name?"

"Nameless," I said. "It's called 'No Name'."

Rosalie was annoyed. She was trying to dress me up, not down.

"My angel has a name," she said. She showed me a faceless little doll made out of lumps that had only a comic smile for a feature, a sort of stick doll. It had a few patches of cloth on and looked workaday, rough, and ready. It was very inexpensive.

I took her over to the most expensive counter where the angelic dolls dressed in gold lame with crepe hoop wings in white were sitting with beatific smiles, as if they were dancing to the music of paradise.

"Here," I said. "I'll buy you this."

"No," she said. "It costs too much."

Rosalie looked at the beautiful doll wistfully with its plastic face. It even had an antique look.

"My angel is not your everyday angel," she said. "She's out there though. She doesn't just blop around. She's not meditating. She's practical. She doesn't fly around and flap her wings over nothing. Something happens, and swoosh, down she comes!"

Part Two

Bread and Butter Blonde

I called Rosalie my bread and butter blonde, to distinguish her from platinums, or broads, girls into gender, college grads, golfers, beady-eyed brunettes, groupies, two-seat beavers, teens, redheads, Sarah Lawrence girls, girls in jeans and tank tops, glamour girls, models, girls with glasses, career women, feminists, your usual housewife, wallflowers, call girls, and whores.

A bread and butter blonde was one who knew value.

It's what you got on your plate before ordering the veal parm.

Value to her was what nuts and bolts might be to a man, but it meant she had her head screwed on.

It was something good.

Something blonde - like bread and butter.

The Sugarmoon

After I got to know her, I thought of taking her to Sicily - to somewhere else.

Here, where we were, was good enough - after all, it was America: and we both wanted liberty and the pursuit of happiness, but something else too - to get away, somewhere beautiful, somewhere to make love and dream, on a boat, perhaps, without interference of, say, the police, where it was like we once hoped it would be.

So I suggested Sicily.

She was very angry.

It was, after all, a college trip; she would have to be with the Alumni. But she didn't say a thing. She just smiled. I thought she was smiling because she wanted the trip, so I paid my money, a big sum, but little did I know: all she wanted was the ring!

I hadn't even bought the ring.

It was only as departure approached that I began to get fidgety, as if something were missing, and I got a strange urge to go to Tiffany's and buy her the canary diamond, the one I had seen with her originally in Big City, on which she had offered me a discount. She was not really greedy. It was a smaller version, something her size, because she wasn't a big woman, no, just a size four, and I thought, after all, if she had no ring, whom would the Alumni think she was?

Nobody. That's whom they would think she was. And it wasn't fair. This was a girl who had no greed in her heart, but a dream.

Myself, I didn't care. I might be a crazy millionaire, a fabulist, but I was nobody too. True, I had paid for the trip and I was, after all, an Alumnus; she hadn't gone to college, so I was trapped. I walked across town in a pretty good mood because I didn't realize what I was doing. How did I know that I was acting out her dream? I thought I was going to buy the ring and that would be the end of it; she would be someone, we would go on the trip, the Alumni would think she was somebody, and everybody would be happy. But that's not the way it worked out.

"This is very romantic," the girl at Tiffany's said. She had honey blonde hair, long red nails, and blue eyes.

"It's his next toy," the senior clerk said sarcastically as I looked with astonishment at the ring.

It was perfect. It looked like my golden girl, only it cost four times as much and more than I had dreamed of spending and was much, much, much more than the discount price she had offered for herself.

Then the girl offered me another ring for three times as much more. I began to wonder who *she* was, and before I knew it she began telling me: married only two years, and she showed me *her* ring.

It was small. I couldn't figure out how much it cost. I began to get nervous that I would never go on the trip and, suddenly, felt guilty for not buying the more expensive ring, and, indeed, for buying her a ring at all. It wasn't my fault. I came away from the store terribly let down, but carrying the perfect ring for my girl.

What had I done?

I had the ring in my pocket at the airport when we started the trip. It was in a little velvet black box wrapped in white with a blue ribbon and I thought she would see it bulge in my pants as we boarded our flight, but she didn't notice. She looked as if she didn't know a thing about it, and we had a last happy salad together in the airport before boarding.

But on the flight I surprised her. At least I thought so. Little did I know, and I didn't even find out till we got back from Sicily, that her hostess from Gino's, who claimed to be a flamboyant - meaning clairvoyant - had already told Rosalie that I was going to give her a ring.

So, after the perfunctory tray meal on the plane, and filling out the evaluation sheet about the flight, I pulled out the little black box according to plan.

Then when she took the package I knew immediately that she knew what was in it, and of course I felt cheated because it was very expensive. I should have given it to her in a hat box. I began to feel we would never get to Sicily and that we probably should have never come and that we might never get back.

"What is it?" she said with the same kind of perfunctory emotion with which the hostesses served the perfunctory meal, chicken or beef.

Rosalie didn't even cry. For my money, I thought I would at least get a good cry but, since I was sort of embarrassed that there wasn't much thrill in it for her, I called the hostess and told her we had just got engaged. She was about as interested in that as she had been in serving the supper menu and didn't even smile. Somebody ought to be happy, I thought, so I went to the chief steward and said we had just got engaged and maybe they would like to do a promotion, love in the clouds, take our picture or something, but he was pretty bland too.

"Well," he said, sort of arrogantly, "if you got engaged on the plane maybe you can get married on the boat."

How did he know we were going on a boat?

We were going on a boat in Sicily. I thought he was being a wise guy, and besides, now that she had the ring, everything seemed to have changed - there was no excitement anymore, no hope. A present gone is a thing forever.

But when I got back to my seat, she said, "It's not the ring that matters. It's my manly."

So much for a lot of money. When the other hostess, the one that even smiled a little, brought us little plastic cups of champagne it didn't even taste good.

In the airport she broke down almost completely. She couldn't even speak.

Nobody in their right mind wants to go to Sicily anyway, which is supposed to sink into the sea sometime around the millennium, rocked by some catastrophic earthquake which will wreck all the glorious honeymoons that ever were, ever are, and ever will be.

Even so, we got ourselves together and had some ham and cheese, washed down by beer, and, as if sorting out our lost lives in the airport, looked at the crafts of Bavaria in the duty free shop, with the cuckoo clocks and the little embroidered aprons.

We were visiting Malta first to get to Sicily, and all the way down over the Alps and along the great peninsula and into the sea of the crossroads of civilization she didn't mention the ring again once.

We met the Alumni in Malta, in the capitol, a place called Valetta, flat little rooftops all the color of burnt resin, scarcely any green, an island desert even in May, but she said, "I have never seen anything like this before."

Actually, it was the first sign of surprise that she had shown on the trip, despite the ring, and for a moment I thought we were going to have a good time after all.

She even called it our sugarmoon - what happens before you get married.

The hotel was an old wartime showplace with poofy upholstered chairs in an atrium banked with palm trees and a black grand piano, where nobody sat except the ghosts of the British empire, in invisible khaki and safari outfits and riding crops and ladies in tea satins, with everybody wondering where the bar was, and the melodies of lost tangos, empty ships, and the faint sound of forgotten artillery.

Our quaint Spanish professor, who was leading the Alumni on this sally into the past, with his Cuban wife, gave his first lecture on the ruminations of ruins and the rhetoric of stones.

It was a disaster, because my golden girl couldn't hear him from the back of the room where she sat with her little size four hands folded in some kind of platitude of regret, despair, and irritation.

Then at dinner, Mr. Salisbury, from St. Louis, died over his oysters. He was telling us about his daughter, and his wife, who was deaf, was listening, when all of a sudden his head slumped and splashed into his plate. Most of the Alumni were that old.

The only thing that interested Rosalie was the pool, where the cactus and flowers bloomed.

But the English were there.

What pleased us about Malta was the understatement, the puzzle of strategic power. The falcon that these kind people anciently, according to custom, gave each year to Charles the Fifth was the origin of the Maltese Falcon, a sign of appreciation for the original gift of this island.

At the pool everything changed. Whether it was the desert sky, or the gin and tonic, or the British conservatives in the whirlpool bath, or the ping-pong players, or the Alumni themselves, or the gardens, with their formalities of flowers, or that burnt resin vista of the towns surrounding the greater and lesser harbors, or simply the ring - whatever it was, it was gone - I went back to the room feeling like a different man while she got a tan at the pool.

And not a better man.

Suddenly I could speak no more. We had visited the inland City of the Dead where all was metaphysical silence, and were ruminating on time and stones, and all of a sudden I could not speak anymore.

I became totally silent, like a ruin.

All the good things I had to tell her were gone. I lay like a sick man on my bed in the gorgeous hotel and even the blue bar didn't cheer me up.

Yes, we saw the Maltese Parliament, the Palace of the Knights, the Cathedral of the Knights of Malta, the statue of Baptist John, and the hilly streets of the capitol and even sat in a cafe.

But I wasn't myself.

The past was whispering in me.

At least, I wasn't the self she wanted me to be.

I didn't propose either. Can identity be such a fragile thing, I thought, that in one moment of a foreign place, in one moment of abandon in the City of the Dead, like love, it is gone?

The Hydrofoil

The hydrofoil left Malta at 4:30 in the morning, under a Mediterranean darkness that was spellbinding.

The Alumni were very upset. We bussed down to the water in gloomy silence and the customs police and guards were on hand behind the barriers for our early departure. No one said a word.

We had to file and pass by one by one, boarding the *St. Francis* with the most awful premonitions. It reminded me of my ignominious departure in the night from England, when I was banished by the police into exile on the continent, all the way across the channel to Belgium, and all for being an American and having run afoul of the Home Office. Then Europe seemed on fire. But here all was quiet.

Rosalie still seemed normal.

As we gained speed, the throttle of the vessel driving my heart, we rose on the fins and a last lighthouse loomed amber on the left, softly chiaroscured against the coming luminous dawn.

If I had stayed in Malta, under the sign of the Falcon, it would all be over now; Rosalie would have had the ring to remember me by, to sell against a rainy day, and we would never have visited Sicily.

The hydrofoil cabin was comfortable. No one sat near us. In fact, since leaving the pool at the hotel, I hadn't spoken a word to anyone, not even the Alumni. Tears for the past kept coming to my eyes, welling up out of nowhere, like the sea, and all I noticed was the easy rocking of the vessel as it cut through some small swells.

What Rosalie was thinking no one knows.

But as the light began to rise from the East she was suddenly on her knees. It was difficult to get on your knees in the hydrofoil because the seat in front was in the way, but she managed anyway without getting stuck. It was this agility you noticed about her.

She could squeeze into any situation.

"Will you marry me?" she said, rather matter-of-factly.

I was deeply shocked.

Besides, I thought some of the Alumni might hear. I had no idea what to say. It had just been three days since I gave her the ring.

If God had given me ears to hear the mutterings of the world, and if I thought I understood something of what was going on, I might have said yes. Instead, I looked stonily out to sea. Besides, she was still on her knees.

A Spanish Engagement

I should explain a Spanish engagement. Although I am not Spanish, I learned this wisdom when in Pamplona at the Running of the Bulls.

There the plaza in town is open to everyone, and at dusk the boys and girls spill into the square surrounded by cafes. The boys circle the square clockwise and the girls walk counterclockwise and, walking into each others' gaze, they make a kind of love with their eyes until the one meant for them comes into focus. Then the families agree and for nine years, under the sharp eyes of a *duenna*, the young promised pair court each other with all their wiles until the time is up and the hard bargaining begins. This is why there are so many happy marriages and broken hearts in Spain.

"But you are not Spanish," Rosalie said when I offered her a Spanish engagement. "Besides, one year is already up."

I had always dreamt of being Spanish. My idea of love was to stand under a window and play a guitar. Now I was on my way to Sicily, once ruled by the Spanish kings, and all that sang was the sea.

If I had had my wits about me I would have said yes, but instead I told her, "I am thinking about it."

This seemed for the moment to satisfy her, although I was afraid she would be even madder than she already was and make a scene in front of the Alumni.

Who knows if opportunity strikes more than once? It seems as if love should be a simple thing. A man will not ask for fear of being refused, or accepted, but a woman seems to have no fear and the question is simply like a kiss in the wind, perhaps to find out where the weather comes from.

It jolted me though, and I didn't really come to until Sicily rose from the sea on our left and we disembarked in Catania, under the cone of Etna. The mountain loomed mysteriously up, like an ominous shadow behind the smog of the city and the drab yellow walls of uneven tenements, as we caught our bus.

Sometime would the world blow up and become a cloud of pumice like this moment threatened to do? She was quiet. From time to time she looked at her ring. How could she know why I was silent? How could she know the cause of the tears?

Then we began passing the fields and hills of vines and lemons and the olive patches, where the hand of God has left no furrow unturned and no piece of earth unhallowed. She murmured, "And I thought my country was beautiful!"

Could I tell her I cried for America? No.

But I even held her hand. The other Alumni sat stiff and grim and motionless in the bus unmoved by anything they saw and apparently as unseeing as they had seemed to be when I was at college as a student. The poetry of it all passed by the windows of the bus without a remark.

"Why don't you say anything to them?" Rosalie asked. "You haven't said a word to anybody. Why did you come on this trip?"

"For the sun, sand, salt and sea," I said.

"Yes," she said, "and you forgot the sex."

The Alumni brightened for some reason when we reached the boat. This was in a village without a name on the southern coast, but the first thing anybody said was, "The boat looks awfully small."

They all expected Aristotle Onassis' yacht. In fact, the ship was Greek, but it was a catamaran, newly appointed, and we boarded without incident to the announcement that the ship would run an open bar because of the early morning departure, which brought smiles to the Alumni, almost shouts of pickled glee, and like little children they ran and strutted about as if luxury were the solution to life.

Then came the fire drill.

She and I had a cabin down in the hold of one of the pontoons on starboard side, and ran up for the mandatory drill. Everybody was atopsides with their orange life vests.

We strapped up and stood around while the captain and crew inspected us until he came to me. He was holding a new life vest and smelled like salt and in one of those clairvoyant moments of life that no one can ever explain he handed me the vest and took mine off and said, "Here, this is your replacement," and he looked at Rosalie.

It made me think of my former wife, and the tears came to my eyes again in astonishment that life could save me twice, drowning in love, yet I was still standing here on deck with the Greek Captain who looked exactly like my former wife's new husband, and how was I to tell all this to Rosalie when she had never even been on a ship before?

But it was that night.

After the Greek music and the love, she broke down for the first time into a crumpled body wracked by tears herself, sobbing as much as when she had made love and holding on to me like a life vest, and yet at the same time accusing me of having tricked her.

The two of us were an operatic mess. If the Alumni had ever seen us we would have been thrown overboard. That was how it was.

Never had a girl changed so fast. From waitress and mother and marathon runner to a corpse of tears and without any rhyme, or reason, except my muteness.

Besides, she was so abusive that I didn't know where to hide.

All because I hadn't said yes?

It was a queen bed with a porthole and a vestibule with the head and a closet, and I almost called the Captain. Maybe there was a spare cabin aboard where I could retire and end the engagement in decency and privacy.

I decided to sleep curled up on the love seat in the vestibule, with its marine blue cushions, and try to sort out the future tomorrow. But she wouldn't let me.

She came out like a little dog and lay down at my feet on the floor with a pillow and nothing I could do would get past her. For some reason the Alumni seemed vastly amused when we appeared together for breakfast and even the quaint Spanish professor who was leading the trip brushed past me with a hitherto unsuspected camaraderie and called me 'Amigo.'

That morning I had prunes, honey, and an egg on top for breakfast.

The ship broke port and headed west.

The Banquet

Rosalie and I had agreed, on our first real date, to some time be buried together.

It was not long afterwards that I began to think about the urn.

According to my plan, our ashes would be mixed; whoever died first buying the urn and willing it to the other to keep until dying into it. We had worked out the original deal at the Hideaway in the Big City while dancing away the night, drinking Greek wine, and looking into each other's eyes.

"You'll be on the bottom of the urn, and I'll be on top," she had said brightly, as if also longing for the day.

But then she changed.

"You have things backwards," she complained. She meant I was planning arrangements for the urn before even getting married. Yet she liked the idea. It was, as yet, her only contract, until I gave her the ring.

The thought of a common urn, in fact, made us both happy.

Eternity would be ours. Final things are easier than the here and now. As it was turning out, the ring was the mistake - not the urn. The plan was to buy an urn in Palermo.

Our next stop was Trapani, where we had a picnic on the way back from Segesta. In Agrigento, we walked on to a movie set.

It was a nameless, interlinear movie in which the starlet walked in and out of romance with the tour guide of a bus, among the temples. They were making a movie within a movie with the making of a movie being the story of a love affair on the one hand, and the romance with the guide being the movie on the other hand. A movie about making a movie, and the villain of the piece was the girl's own husband, and finally, after lovely shots of the famous temple, one saw her dead naked body stretched on the beach and the husband and the bus guide shaking hands and kissing each other on the check in the eucalyptus trees behind the dunes.

Rosalie looked just like the starlet.

I remember her walking in front of the temple. It could have been a tracking shot, from left to right, moving as if on screen and carefully, as if something - the guide maybe - was around the corner, vanishing to the right, as if off screen.

A perfect walk. Full of a kind of fervor. A trailer of something to see, a coming attraction. It was interlinear itself, between the past of the temple, and the movie she had never been in, was not in, would never be in. But Rosalie had real talent.

Afterward we had a picnic, on a wall down by the sand, a bus picnic that was a sacrifice to the gods of humdrum sandwiches - yet the sand was real, and the sea. We were climbing back to the bus when I saw the perfect urn.

It was a slender vase in burnt orange and black, on a peddler's stand with figures and a horse, two handles; the urge to buy it was immediate.

No peddler would ship an urn and I couldn't carry our death pot in my hands for the rest of the day with the Alumni right there.

It wasn't until Palermo, in fact, that I saw another urn that was right.

Paiermo is set on a fluvial flat coming out of the mountains and is a black city of three languages and the night. That was when we saw it.

The tenements stretched straight and endless on seamy streets, with only a little gold. The port dominated the town, in which shadows of suggestion lurked from an edgy present. People were everywhere, but indeterminate, as if they didn't know the reality to which they belonged.

I had planned to walk here from the ship to Via Vittorio Emmanuel and sit in a cafe near the cathedral, wearing my black shirt and black tie and drinking campari, but once I saw the place I knew I would be lost immediately.

None of this phased Rosalie. She wore a tidy little outfit in blue, and we went to dine at a palace by special invitation in the Old Quarter, which looked like a piece of eaten stone on the outside.

When we got to the palace, we passed through the courtyard and up the travertine steps into the foyer, adorned with lilies and portraits. I had brought a piece of marzipan fruit as a gift, but Rosalie glared me down and I put it on a sideboard out of the way without ever giving it to the princess.

Two Sicilian ladies came to greet us. It was an embarrassing moment. No one knew which one was the princess. It could have been either. Then one of them gave a little speech and the Alumni were very pleased with themselves.

The place was genteel, and after we were ushered in I shook hands with the prince. He was a motley, ash-colored fellow with a ragged unshaven look, half-smoked to death in a nondescript jacket as if he had just dragged himself in from the tobacco shop. I felt like saying to them that Rosalie was the princess, and in fact the two ladies came over especially and, ignoring me completely, gave her a touching little welcome - which, I thought, was pretty good for a waitress. It was almost the high moment of our trip, except for a moment later.

I looked at some little paintings on the wall, then cornered Rosalie against the mantle after we had both been given drinks.

"Ouch!" she said, and the whole room was looking at us.

I didn't care. She looked just like the starlet at Agrigento and I thought to myself, this is what we came for, an audience with the Gattopardo, the Leopard, played in the movie by Burt Lancaster, a moment of love. I didn't even care about the canapes any longer.

The whole of nobility could be hanged if only they would be the backdrop for her face, and I think the Alumni expected us to dance. That's when I should have proposed. Alas, I didn't, and soon we were ushered into dinner. It was a buffet.

Probably it was the best table she had ever seen. I won't even bother to describe it. She didn't say a word. What can a waitress who slings pizza in Somewhere City, USA say about a menu with the likes of *Sformato di Riso, Involtini di melanzane con fusilli,* and *Tagliatelle con Zucchini Fritti?*

"How much does a meal like this cost?" Rosalie asked when we got back to our table, probably figuring what the twenty per cent tip would be.

Suddenly I saw that it was not the blue dress she had on, but the lemon yellow dress - our color. But I had no time to notice because a very plump young lady with a round face and a gold tooth speaking pidgin English in an elegant way sat down with her plate beside me, and instinctively I

73

knew this was the real princess and that the other ladies were just in waiting, fronts for the real thing.

Should I talk to the waitress or the princess?

So I turned to the princess, the Sicilian one, and said, "I'd like you to meet the princess," and I introduced my golden girl.

To tell you the truth, I was torn between two princesses, and two realities too. One was a princess of the heart, and the other a princess of title.

My old allegiance was to the Sicilian aristocrat girl on my right, and my new allegiance was to Princess Rosalie, the girl on my left.

Meanwhile, I was trying to eat my *tagliatelle*.

In fact, I had nothing to say.

But Rosalie kept elbowing me and saying, "Why don't you talk to her?"

The City of the Dead was still haunting me.

Finally, I told Rosalie that supper cost $500 and that that was the way these aristocrats made their living, which gave my girl some kind of satisfaction.

When it came to dessert, I gave the Sicilian princess my arm, but my heart was by this time with the fiction of Princess Rosalie, that is, the waitress. But I turned my back on Rosalie and paraded off to the buffet table with the Sicilian, thinking how easy it would have been, with the right introductions, to have married her instead of the waitress, if that was what I was ever going to do - but my girl then taught me a lesson.

"Which one is the *cassata?*" she said in an acid tone when we got back to the table.

Then she said under her breath, "So, are you going to fuck her?"

Sicilian cassata is made of ricotta, not of ice cream,

and I didn't just pretend to be confused. The strawberry ice cream was as good as anything I ever tasted but I said to the Sicilian, "My daughter-in-law sings in the opera. Maybe she could sing in Palermo?"

And she said, "We'll think about it."

A pretty neat piece of business. It's not everyday you travel to Palermo and get your daughter-in-law considered for the Sicilian opera.

Then came the *limonella* liqueur.

By this time I was in a pretty miff because Rosalie the waitress and I were going into the urn together, when I could have been staying here eating *gelato* and associating with the real people of Palermo, and waltzing in the banquet room of the palace and having those lemon trees and olive groves and maybe even owning a temple, but I must say the *limonella* snapped me out of my mood.

I thought of my grandfather as I sipped it with her, and imagined all the New England ancestors looking on as I toasted the future of the urn with my waitress.

Then Rosalie said, "Now that you've fallen for the princess, why don't we get out of here?"

Exits are always difficult and of course I wanted to tell the Sicilian princess and her people that it was the best banquet my waitress had ever had, and reminded me of my grandfather, but Rosalie said: "I saw you giving her your arm. You'd just like to screw her right here in front of everybody, wouldn't you? Well you can't. You're my man, and they can't have your perfect little body. So there."

Actually, I wanted another glass of *limonella*. That, and to talk to my grandfather.

But I got up, as if on cue, and went straight out into the foyer, turned left, down the marble stairs, across the courtyard, to the door with its electronic latch, and, as if I were the prince, nodded to the guard and they let me out into the night.

Rosalie was not far behind.

An alley cat from Palermo ran up and then hid behind a bicycle wheel. The light was dim. A garbage van with yellow lights went by.

As usual, I thought this was my last chance to walk off, unknown, into the darkness.

And to never come back.

The Brioche

The other perfect urn we saw was also in Palermo. It was the next day.

One of those smooth tourist buses with the gliding German ride took us up early on to the Conca d'Oro, Palermo's Gold Coast, a high up valley ridge on the west of the city and reaching back into the fertile, magic slopes of the inner island where the lemons and orchards grow in a kind of baroque munificence that is horticultural - real, that is - yet also a painted scene on which the people of Sicily thrive.

We were set down in the Square of the Dons and taken into another church where the dim light prevented us from seeing even the altar and only the candles of the dead burned for the departed thoughts that haunt the living.

An electric light in the apse flashed on and off periodically, lighting up the mosaics, and then dimmed, leaving us brooding about whether light was truth, or truth was light. *Lux et Veritas*. It was a moment of exotic recollection for the Alumni.

Here, Rosalie wasn't bothering me. She had never seen anything of the kind, and a marriage was taking place.

Her reaction to this was a puzzle to me. She seemed totally absorbed in the ceremony as if I didn't exist. Yet she held on to my hand. I wanted to kiss her. The marble stones were right for love, perfect for dancing. I began my little routine, one two three cha cha cha, feeling lithe and supple as the unheard music drew me out towards freedom, and I took her arm.

"There's no dancing in church," she told me, oblivious of how I felt.

The engagement, in fact, was drawing us further apart and as she fixated on the bride and groom, the black and white of the universe of their formality, I shattered inside like a window and thought of a dancer throwing away her shoes, red shoes, to never dance again, as if youth were over before it began and all our dreams were doomed to die before the music even started.

It was she, in fact, who had introduced me to the ballroom and the cha cha cha of eternity to the sound of post modern swing, and now, here she was, in Palermo, telling me not to dance in church.

It was not like at the airport waiting for the shuttle, when we danced on the sidewalk and the big black guy driving the limousine said with a laconic smile, "I don't hear the music." That had been Big City. Was Palermo so different?

The Leopard's last waltz with his son's bride in the palatial grandiosity of the Conca d'Oro above the Sicilian capitol came back to me, and his lingering glance back from the memories of aristocracy and the Old Order toward the effervescence of his youth, as the last century died - and here I was standing in the same place with a waitress. Outside, the lemon trees with small white flowers were in bloom and a redolence of fragrant aroma, the perfume of an island, hung in the air.

It reminded me of how we had met. I was on the way back from another wedding, after which the bride, on the morning after, left a note to her groom that she had made a mistake and walked out to join another man - a wedding we had all believed in - and I had sat down in seat number 23A, still parked on the runway minding my own business and trying to put together the tattered remnants of my soul. I saw Rosalie in the aisle poised like a squirrel, or perhaps, in her beige striped linen suit, a little like a rumpled night owl, something terribly wise about the eyes as if the sad smile of life had left footprints in the flesh, and crisp, yes, crisp. But you couldn't tell how old she was, or if she was young, maybe, and without a further thought I said to her, "Sit down and talk to me."

"That seat is taken," she said.

"No it's not," I answered.

She straddled my knees and in no time, to my astonishment, was sitting beside me talking in a Brooklyn accent, and I would never have guessed in a million years that she was not only foreign but also crying because she was going back home to America.

Years of despair gushed up in me and I began talking a blue streak, amazed that she listened, that she answered, that she was there.

Seven hours flashed by like nothing and even when we landed I still did not know she was a waitress.

She offered to carry my bag when we arrived but something came over me in the airport and as we approached customs I saw her again as a stranger walking into the future away from me and didn't know whether to be happy or sad or just follow her through the terminal to the end of time. We didn't even say goodbye. We just became terminal strangers. The thing was scary.

But I had given her my name.

Now it was months later and we were in Palermo getting an urn.

We walked, in Palermo, out into the sunlight and headed across the Square of the Dons to a ceramic shop and I saw the urn there. It was plain terracotta, about knee high, shaped like an amphora, and standing just outside the shop being used as an ashtray.

"This is just it," I said, holding it up for her to see. "It's perfect."

I think it was in this moment that she had second thoughts, because the next time I talked to her about our ashes being mingled for ever she said she wanted two urns - the one we had seen on the peddler's wagon, with the figures, for her, and this one, the plain one, for me.

I was devastated.

The dream we had hatched in the Hideaway was smashed and all the pain of the years without her and of the indeterminacy of the future was reborn in an instant. I begged her to explain why, suddenly, it was to be two urns instead of one.

"Because we'd be reborn twins," she said at first.

But there was a darker reason. She had someone else in mind.

She didn't want her dust to be violated with mine, to become one, because in the shadow world of the future life she still wanted to be herself in case this other person wanted her.

Yet, in this life, she wanted to be married.

I was stumped. If you want to be one flesh in this world, why hedge your bets against the next one?

There was something going on here that I didn't understand, something not even a priest could explain, and all I could do was follow her across the square to a cafe with bright tables and sunshine and order a *cappuccino* and a *brioche* stuffed chock full with juicy green fried peas that melted in my mouth.

After all, this, and the urn, was what I had come for.

She sat there like a cipher and watched me eat.

The Girl in Blue

Our next stop was Cefalu.

In Palermo, I had given her three choices. Fly home, continue the trip, or ask for political asylum in Sicily.

As a waitress, of course, she couldn't work in Italy, or, for that matter, Sicily, so I would have to provide. If I changed my name I couldn't get my funds out of the United States, and I couldn't count on the Sicilians to provide a villa and a lemon grove.

Working for the Mafia was the only alternative and all I could do would be to teach them English as a second language. This is better paid in Sicily than in the United States, but still, it would have meant one of those dingy apartments down by the docks and I knew she didn't want to live there.

I swallowed hard, and, with the Alumni, we went on to Cefalu.

The Professor gave his second lecture.

We were at sea, and I ordered up an *ouzo* on the rocks with soda and sat alone. One of the Alumni ladies came over and made a pleasantry, and I said a few words to her, that I can't remember, and then she rejoined her party and I overheard her lady friend saying, "Did he say anything?"

She nodded assent, as if she had scored some tremendous victory, and I did not know at the time one of the Alumni, in fact, a whole little clique of them, were already planning to sue the travel agency because they thought the whole trip was rotten.

They didn't like the drinks. They didn't like the upholstery in the ship's lounge. They thought the cabins were cramped and lousy. They didn't like the buses. They didn't like the ruins. The sun was too strong. The food was Greek. There were no cards to play and no bridge in the lounge. There was no television.

They had a thousand reasons, including the one that they would not admit: they didn't really like each other or themselves and they only came on the trip to get away from themselves, and all that they had found in the Mediterranean was themselves. It was the same old story.

The Professor, instead, was on form, dressed tightly in a dark jacket and black and white check pants that trimmed a little too much on his squat, swarthy body, a regular Pancho decked out as a professor with a thick, flaky accent, a mixture of Cuban and Basque, and dark eyes - not blue at all.

His subject was ruins.

"Ruminations of regret," he said, "are the remnants of our remembrance. We savor the sea's tintinnabulations as salt corrodes the stone of our structure, but it was Petrarch first who discovered time in the self, the self as a tune, and stone as the seminary of the mind. This was the first Western University.

"We are in the thirteenth century sitting on the border of the beyond, when suddenly the stones speak, and it is this speaking that we still hear today. From the silence of the lizards' tongues in the sun. Then the Baroque builds a manner on Petrarch's discovery, and the view broadens from the plain of prose into the monuments of eternity. But there is no way back. The soul is trapped in its own discovery. Until we come to modernity, and there we discover the ruins again, the ruins inside ourselves, the ruins of ourselves."

He looked around at the Alumni. Some had their chins on their canes in deep thought. The women especially were interesting to watch.

As for myself I felt deeply ashamed.

Rosalie hadn't even bothered to come.

Her thesis was entirely different from the Professor's. In her view, she had a body - as she said, she didn't need a Bergdorf Goodman dress because she was a person and could dress better than the Alumni on $27 and a few stitches. In fact, she could sew.

The Alumni might be ruins, but she wasn't going to listen to it. That would only tear down everything she believed. It might be culture, this ruin stuff, but it didn't help you wait on tables. Rosalie wasn't a ruin.

When somebody is eating, they don't want a ruin waiting on them, they want spunk. A little class.

They want their drinks and their food, a little look from behind after the meal has been served. A waitress has to be someone, not just a ruin, or say anything that comes into her head.

"They're all jealous of my body," she told me as we left Palermo behind.

The boat headed out from Palermo, southern capital of the lemon tree, a fluvial plain of tenements and villas, a clouded urbanity of Sicilian elegance, and left the wake of the boat in the late sun shining in silver and sparkling in gold.

It was a sad moment for all of us. It seemed like a city bristling with opportunity, a dark promise, a venue of escape.

It was here that leisure beckoned and relief from the metropoli of the West, a place to sip campari and taste the bitter sweet earth of death.

We had not bought the urns.

The moment of our mingling seemed past, as if some promise had been broken, and death, instead of uniting us, would now part us. It was as if at the temple of Segesta some rite had separated us and now our pact to live together was under the strain of being single - of individuality.

Everything brightened in Cefalu.

The yacht headed into the small port on a headland that divided the town in two, a castle to the east, like an outlook, and the church to the west nestled in the village of stucco, the mountains of Sicily behind.

In my deckchair gazing out at the sea lapping against the port I felt like Franklin Delano Roosevelt, a man without legs, travelling in the mind across the waters of destiny to this isolated spot. It was as if I had some affair of State to complete in unknown waters, with my girl behind the wheelchair.

"That's where I want to live," she said, pointing up high on the escarpment above the village to the villa in earthen orange with a terrace to the sea.

As we approached, someone aboard the yacht sang the song of the girl from Cefalu: *her heart in blue, whom I remembered yonder over the years when I left her true.*

It was an emigrant song about a wanderer who had left this port maybe fifty years ago, his girl behind, and probably never came back, but remembered her waving goodbye when he left for another life.

I wished I had been him, returning.

Rosalie wished she were the girl from Cefalu.

The police, customs, and village hands were on the landing as we came in because in Cefalu nothing else happens: birth, death, a song or two, and a visit to Palermo is all that life offers and a view of the sea.

This was what Rosalie wanted.

We disembarked and started walking up the pier to the road into town, without luggage, without care, the blue yacht in the background with the Alumni hugging the harbor, and our souls lightened as if we would walk away into eternity right here and never come back.

But halfway to the village I had second thoughts.

She wanted to go on. Suddenly she began pulling me by the arm, wrestling with me, even hitting me. I wouldn't go another step.

It was as if around the corner fate awaited.

If I went into town with her it would be irretrievable. I would at last be the nobody I threatened to be and yet it scared me as much as being the somebody I already was, even more.

"Can't you even take just a walk?" she said scathingly.

The bystanders began to laugh, not knowing whether we were embracing or fighting, and a charter bus by the wayside peered jeeringly at us.

"The Alumni are having cocktails," I said pathetically, feeling all the manhood drain out of me.

"They'll wait," she replied. "They want to drink to our engagement."

"They don't even know we're engaged," I answered, tearing myself loose and heading back to the ship.

A smile broke over her face.

It was kind of victory for the girl from Cefalu, a kind of final vengeance for all that this forgotten girl might have suffered in the fifty years that her man was away.

Under Rosalie's withering gaze, I knew that, just as I didn't have the courage to stay here forever, to just walk away from it all, I never would have had the courage to leave Cefalu in the first place. America was too far, too lonely, too scary.

Rosalie was aglow in my discomfort.

Know thyself.

The wisdom of the temples.

The Blue Hotel

Amalfi was our last stop. That's where we danced together, when it seemed for the last time, by the sea.

Amalfi lies like a pearl in an oyster on the coast above Salerno, a port of hotels and honeymoons and nights aglitter by the sea.

Our hotel was a five-star cluster of rooms on seven levels with elevators down to the pool and crystal blue water.

It was a diadem of Mediterranean luxury with terraces, balconies, and lemon trees. Our room had the biggest balcony of all, a terrace for dancing above the sea, as if music were wrapped in plastic like a muffled piano behind the balustrade. We longed for the night. For the stars.

The only thing wrong was that the room smelled worse than a dead fish. A putrid odor emanated from it as if all the sewage of the charter weddings from all time rose into one's nostrils and all the food ever eaten on those honeymoons was rotting under the floor. It was almost impossible to breathe. But management had left us a plate of fresh fruit.

Besides, the ring didn't fit.

It may have been in Amalfi that she first got the idea of selling it because, as she said, it was the man that was important - not the ring.

"You just think that with the ring you can do a little delaying action," she said over supper, as in the next room a newlywed couple in black and white sipped, supped, and began to dance the evening away.

The last thing that had ever come to my mind was that I might be more important than a ring. It was a stumper all right, and I just wished we were back in Palermo.

My silence irked her too.

We began having one way conversations in which only she spoke and all the things I had said to her for a year became a monument of the past.

"You tricked me," she repeated. "You pretended. And now you don't have a word to say."

Since visiting the Silent City in Malta, the City of the Dead, I had lost my tongue, and all the things I wanted to say to her - all the things I had said to her - were like a monstrous joke dooming our relationship and making the future heavy with gloom.

If this was our engagement, what would marriage be? Yet already she was looking for a wedding dress.

"The answer," she said, "is yes, yes, *yes!*"

It made no sense. Yet we dressed up and walked down the narrow roadway running along the embankments of the mountains into town and as I walked behind her, though she was a waitress, I couldn't help thinking that she had it all over the Alumni and their women because she had the motion.

It was as simple as that: the motion. It came not from breeding, from finishing schools, from money, from the Ivy League, from college graduation - it came from waiting on tables, from slinging all that pizza, and from the $18 bargain dress.

Part Three

So Long Cefalu

After we got back, I didn't even know why we had gone. I remembered her sobbing in my arms to the Greek music down in the hold, not knowing whether to call the tour guide, the Captain, or whom - she shook so, as if her world had ended, and when we got back she said coldly, matter-of-factly, "We've had our time. Our time is over..."

I had heard this before. But not so soon. I mean not two weeks after the engagement. In fact, it felt so alien to my ears that in a moment I believed it. Truth is always a surprise.

I didn't care about the ring. The ring was hers. I cared about her heart, and she was no longer mine. Not one urn anymore, but two.

It seemed like a real tragedy, now, that we had not gotten off the ship forever in Cefalu. But we were home - so to speak. We even got a refund for the trip.

The money was like some bitter joke, as if denying that we had ever been on our sugarmoon.

It was money that said: *the music was not real, the landscape you saw was not real, the sea you swam in was not real, the love you made was nothing.*

It was as if the Alumni, with all their complaints and gripes, all their minor bellyaches, all their memories of college and cocktails and making little pleasantries about the weather this, and the weather that, and golf, and television, all the things they liked to talk about, had won the final victory over Sicily and we had never seen the moon, and the waves, and the lemon groves.

Besides, I was now engaged in a relationship that was over, committed to a love that was gone, involved with a waitress who no longer dreamed of being buried in an urn with me, mingling our ashes forever, but wanted to be married.

To make matters worse, I had stopped talking entirely.

No matter what she said, I couldn't think of a word fast enough to say.

Furthermore, our photos came out badly.

There were no shots of two dangerous and beautiful people on a sugarmoon in foreign waters, tempting fate, looking longingly into each others' eyes, hanging on the abyss, looking at the moon, holding each others' hands ready to jump into the Aegean for their lives. All the photos showed were blimpy, ugly, bulbous selves, without even a smile, staring glazed and angry and bitter at the camera while Rosalie sat alongside, pretty as ever, laughing, or trying to laugh.

It had seemed like a dream shining in tears when we were there, with the glitter of the sea, and all the photos showed were the ruins of dreams and a few temples.

She smuggled home three lemons. That was all.

As for our bags, they were missing at the airport. Not only the car keys, but the house keys were in the bag, and she had to be at work the next day.

It was twelve at night.

Either we could stay in a hotel, or take the cab sixty miles to her house, the tract home in Somewhere City, USA, which now seemed our only refuge. So long Cefalu! I was locked out.

Welcome home.

The Return

After our return, I had grave doubts about myself. There was a cartoon in a magazine that pictured a man on his knees, and she was saying to him, "Carl, are you really proposing or have you simply stopped taking your medication?"

Rosalie reverted back to her diminutive speech and, as a result, we stopped speaking English and began to talk a kind of pidgin language. For instance, I began to say, "Whatly do you have to eatly?" and things like that.

She also had unusual expressions, like when she was angry she would say, "Oh, you're full of prunes," or, "You're full of fruit."

In a word, her speech was polished and elocuted so that it had a kind of enchantment about it, as if some bird like a parrot had gotten into some other bird's nest, and made a little melody out of someone else's whistle.

For me, she talked like a parody, a wonderful burlesque of the American dialect, making it sound like an elite cabaret piece of business.

It was sort of Marlene Dietrich doing a rendition of the Bronx, with her tongue and legs showing all the time. I couldn't get enough of it. All she had to do to make me smile was open her mouth.

She could say words like *car*, and *bar*, and *far*, and I

would break up. She had all the vowels down perfect, only so that all the sloppiness was gone, yet the slanginess was intact, as if someone had polished a steel cafeteria knife.

She couldn't sing at all, yet she carried a tune in near perfect pitch. When she sang, she looked like a small monkey, the kind that used to collect the money when the accordion man played.

She mugged it up too. Like a monkey, she had little elastic lips that she swallowed so that she had no mouth left, and it was as if she were wearing a stocking over her face.

Then she would say, "Whatly?"

But her real talent was still dancing. She had never had a ballet lesson in her life, so that when she did a pirouette, it was a pretty strange little contortion, but she was doing it all the time. It looked like a comedienne that no one has seen before, all akimbo, and her little arms would fly out off balance and she would imitate her head up in the air like a classical monkey.

Her legs were very good. Not dancer's legs, but athlete's legs - this was because she had run the marathon, and her weight was not in her head, but in the calves, where she could stand like an acrobat on a wire and push and hold herself down to earth.

There was none of this floating off kind of thing, or wafting the arms around in empty space. In fact, she was like a top once she got going; all she needed was a little push and she went off into a trot that would never stop like some kind of little engine piston in a lawn mowing machine. She had the rhythm all right - and the motion.

These things only made me love her more, but as soon as we got back she started trying to get me to pin down the date for the wedding. All the fun and agreement we had had about a Spanish courtship lasting for nine years was forgotten.

She tricked me into going back to Tiffany's to size the ring I had given her, but it was actually an excuse to try on wedding bands.

Another thing she had on her mind was doing over my house. What she wanted was to move out of Somewhere City, USA, where she lived in her tract house, and move the whole thing exactly as she had it, upholstery, poofs, and all, into Big City where I had my office and domestic arrangements.

In fact, I only had one closet and a day bed, and though it was fine for me, she wanted to change all that. She also wanted to convert the library into a living room and the small front gallery I had into a kitchen, tear down the partitions, and get rid of the day bed where I snoozed.

She wanted to bring all of her photographs with her, the family photos and shots of the girls at Gino's, framed, that lined her tables, kitchen, and the parlor - there were fifty-nine of them, I counted - and put them instead of the paintings and books.

"I love you dearly the way you are," she said, "so now change!"

I still wasn't talking after coming back from the City of the Dead, so we would have conversations like: "Don't you want to go for a walk?"

"No, I don't want to go for a walk," she answered.

"Ow, my God," she exclaimed.

"You're sure you don't want something to eat?" she asked.

"No? No walk?" she said.

"What are you thinking?" she asked.

"No? Not thinking anything?" she said.

"I love you!" she exclaimed.

"Three words. Just three words. You could say them. Why don't you get down on your hands and knees and say them?" she said.

"No?" she said.

"Whatly?" she whined.

And it would go on for days this way.

Yet she still promised to keep her promise, and be buried in the urns together - but she wanted one thing clear; she was going to be the ashes on top.

I was to be the first to go.

The Free Market

Over dinner one night, I asked Rosalie about why she always judged things and people on their appearance.

"What?" I asked, "Is the difference between the inside and the outside of a thing? How can you tell?"

I was looking for a deep discussion, like: what is the relation between mind and matter, maybe, or how you identify value. Do you trust your instincts? Your judgement?

Rosalie scoffed.

"What you see is what you get," she said. And she meant it. She was her own apparition, that way; you dressed, not to kill, but to suit the circumstance. She was always right for the occasion.

"You mean the outside and the inside are the same?" I asked.

"Appearances are everything?"

She parried this one too.

"I may not read books, but I'm smart," she answered. And she made her monkey face, swallowing her mouth.

Like a little rhesus monkey, jumping from tree to tree, she was fast, Rosalie was, with her body language; she didn't always need a tongue.

"Look," she said, "don't pick on me. I cook. I clean. I sew. I launder. What do you do?" Then she tried to brush my hair back and fluff it up.

"Your hair is going every which way," she said. "You shouldn't comb it back that way. Leave it natural. You look a hundred per cent better."

"I made good money last night," Rosalie said again, and she would still wonder where I made my money.

"I grub on the street," I finally answered. "I find money in the gutters."

It was a crazy millionaire's answer.

True, I found pennies on the street and always bent over to pick them up. True, I had been homeless, almost panhandling.

But what I looked for were ideas on the street, like scraps of old newspapers. Some inspiration from the shop windows, all glass and concrete.

I hung out in convenience stores cadging the free coffee samples and reading the newspapers free, I cased corporation skyscrapers and plants along the industrial parks. I was a freelancer; whatever I learnt I tried to translate into a profit on the Street - in this case: Wall Street.

So it was true, I was grubbing on the street, looking everywhere for earnings, and trying to cash in on the Free Market.

Back to Gino's

Something always drew her back to Gino's. Even on a night off, she'd drift back to the place, and when we ate out, I'd ask her, "Where would you like to go?"

Silence. Then, "We could go to Gino's."

If I said yes, she would brighten up.

"I'll get dressed," she would say. "What should I wear?"

"You know I never tell you what to wear."

"But I want to please you."

Actually, she was thinking of how she would look in Gino's.

Mostly she already knew what she would wear. The money she made went from Gino's straight over to Lucky Lady, where she would buy the name labels from the rack for a pittance.

"We can have the veal parm," she would add - it was still the customer's most favorite dish.

How many times had she served it? Sixteen years is a long time through the swinging doors. Count it for yourselves - that's around seventy-five thousand trays. She was a slip of a girl too.

And there were four steps up to the station on the mezzanine.

"Maybe Dolly will be on. I think so," she said, looking forward to curling up in the booth and having our drinks.

"But the eggplant is awfully good too," she said, as if she hadn't seen enough of it.

She always walked in like a lady, almost as if she had never seen the place before.

"No, no," she objected to my taking a booth, "we have to wait for the hostess."

She had often served the Mudslide from the bar, but never had one. A lugubrious sweety of creme de cacao and mint and cream, she ordered one.

"I'm having the mudslide," she said. "I've never had one. I have to show off my gorgeous one," she added, referring to no less than me.

Little could these girls know whom they were meeting - a fabulist, after all, is one who believes that truth is in fiction, in escaping from the bubblegum culture into the imagination.

As the girls came by with their trays they said, "Hi!" and, if they had time, shook hands. They had heard all about me in the kitchen, of course. They made out like I was new, scarcely looking at me, telling Rosalie the latest news.

Shoulder to shoulder for years, tray to tray, and they all belonged to the Freedom Club - freedom from Gino's. The girls' club.

I, in my shiny clothes, because Rosalie always insisted I spiff up, was meeting 'the girls.'

The girls did this, the girls said that - I felt like I knew them all together, but none of them alone. They were the rank and file, the collective, but inside each of them was a Rosalie.

"I made good money tonight," Rosalie always repeated after a turn.

Tonight I was spending the good money. It was like

being on the other side of the desk, the other side of the altar, the other side of the kitchen door - only Rosalie wouldn't have to cash in.

I was supposed to tip big. Ten per cent was puny. Even twenty per cent was not enough. These were the girls. Twenty-five per cent at least.

For Rosalie, Gino's was a kind of reward. Like being in the movie you had made, or being on the other side of the mirror. It gave her a sense of satisfaction to be served in Gino's as if all those years had led to something.

She carefully read the menu she knew by heart, and ordered the gorgonzola salad. She listened to the specials she could herself recite but already knew what to order. It was like eating on the other side of her own reflection. I was the customer she had won.

"Marla is slow," she would say, watching the girls. "She can't do her tables."

Or, "That one is new. She won't last long."

"You should relax," I said. "Enjoy your meal. You're on this side of the table now."

"I know," she answered. "I like coming to Gino's, don't you?"

Hard work, and that beatific smile.

The Money

I was a crazy millionaire, a fabulist, she knew, but as she said, "One of us has to work." So she stayed on the job.

Besides, Rosalie was used to living from hand to mouth. The restaurant was an incentive. Every meal was a small lottery.

Sometimes she came out with $36, sometimes with $56, or, if it was supper, it was sometimes $86, sometimes as much as $150.

She didn't follow the stock market, but her job was a financial report on every day. Rosalie was an index unto herself.

Rosalie went up or down with the tips, and after hours she sat at her kitchen table, the bills stacked on one side, the night's earnings on the other side, and she counted out the ones, the fives, the tens against the debts.

She liked to be able to pay down the credit card. But she was always finding new bargain clothes. A dress for $18, a jacket, slacks, a skirt.

It was called Lucky Lady, the bargain store, and because she was a size four, the good clothes fit because, in Somewhere City, USA, everybody almost was larger than Rosalie.

"I have a body," she still liked to say, wriggling into the latest slim fit.

The money mostly was gone before she even needed to get to the bank.

The Dialogue

I enter into the things of life like a character who is the protagonist of the very story that he himself is writing.

This is good both coming and going. It was only a little hard to make it clear to Rosalie.

Rosalie was not a writer. She was not aware of the script. She was not aware of being her own story or the heroine of my story.

She lived, but more as if it were a movie. She was watching herself in a movie. Life was like a mirror. But she hadn't produced, written, and directed it, nor shot the camera. She was acting in it all right, but it wasn't as if she was producing it or had dreamed it up - she was just acting in it.

You could tell. If there was a mirror in the room, she checked each shot.

But she said the dialogue faster than she could ever think it up.

"They shut me off early last night," she reported.

Litany of Love

I could sing: "I got a gal, a car, a pad in town, and spare change - what else can a crazy millionaire want?"

Something, but what?

Love? Rosalie was all the love I needed.

My mind wanted something more. Call it a soul.

A Mount Everest to climb. Like an athlete, a record to break. A hope. Desire. What good is food without hunger?

"Rosalie. What is the soul?"

Life wanted a horizon to sail beyond, an Eldorado to reach, a Glockomora to live in. I wanted to hear a song that I had never heard before, that had that perfect beat. I wanted the motion. The rhythm. I wanted Rosalie - but I still didn't think of getting married.

I wanted to dance all night and see the stars that after death I might travel to; I wanted the perfect walk into the sunset and the fadeout.

I wanted life with Rosalie to be a movie of the spirit with all the suspense and travel of a true film, and the tramp, his life in a satchel, trudging happy into the final dissolve.

I wanted Rosalie's world, but the other world too - the other world informing it now, painting the flowers brighter than real, more present than now.

Bread and wine and love, not for themselves only, but for the bread of life, the wine of remembrance, the love to come. The lunch counter was fine but I wanted it to be an altar at the same time. Even the waitress: a real woman, but a metaphor too, a fable.

She had to be the ethos of America, the waitress: woman serving coffee - but the girl on the cymbal too, the dancing Susanna at the royal procession, the secret mystery, the initiation.

The waitress was Americans' omnipresent answer to the maiden of the seven veils; she stood, she carried, she served. She looked good from behind in the mirror.

But it didn't end with the ponytail and the bubblegum. It didn't end with the coffee cup and the mirror. My world traveled through physical reality into the beyond, the extension of the table, the Alice world behind the mirror, the soul behind the lipstick and smile.

I looked for the poem. The movie.

Without the poem, the words had no meaning.

It wasn't a simple matter of, "Good morning," and, "Have a nice day!" It was a matter of life and death.

Rosalie didn't understand a word of what I was saying.

But material reality wasn't cut and dry; the two by four wasn't just dimensional stuff sixteen feet long: it was a tree. A tree growing in paradise. I wanted it all: the myth with Rosalie, Mary even, and Magdalene, with Mary, Jane, the tree - and Rosalie.

Both rhyme and reason.

I walk in my soul, form of forms. That was it.

Not just one hundred and twenty pounds, five foot four, and thirty-four, twenty-four, thirty-four, but slender as lavender with almond eyes and a thinking air, and behind the body moving through this reality of the world the soul stalking that other reality.

Rosalie and the dream.

The city that was not just a place on a map or a pile of buildings downtown, but also a labyrinth of streets going somewhere - a city that was not just Somewhere City, USA, but also a movie. A city on the hill. A life that was a theater in the dark and I was sitting there and looking at it in lights.

The dancer and the dance.

Not just another evening out for $15.

Not just another click of the surfer on TV.

I wanted reality to be the parable of itself, love to be the flame of the invisible, the sun to be a sacrament of light, and a walk on the street to be a journey to this land of being. And this being to be the fairy tale of beyond.

I didn't want much. The best part of it was free. I wanted what every waitress in America wants. It was simply a question of never giving up hope and hanging on to the dream.

No, I didn't want much - but how to explain it to Rosalie?

"Hmmm," she said. "You want another cup of coffee?"

A Body for a Body

To Rosalie, love meant ironing a man's shirt. She wasn't above it. Political correction hadn't gotten to her, nor gender politics.

Her sense of giving was her body. That was the final value. The last gift.

She could still cook a meal too. Serving her man was still part of her vocabulary. Seating him, dishing up hot food. That was her sense of love, no matter what others said.

A woman was there to tell a man he had a spot on his shirt, or tie. A spot of any kind really exercised Rosalie. She also wanted her man clean, sweet, and spiffy. That was part of going out.

And sewing. She could still darn socks, and sewing a button was part of making love. It was the gesture of the thing. It was her function. It was her way of paying her way - and a good girl paid her way.

It was some old kind of school, some other century of tradition, an outworn custom, her and her manly. It came, for her, with waitressing. It came with serving. It came with being a woman.

She had it from her mother, her mother had it from her mother's mother. But it didn't sit heavy on her. Doing the lunch trick might net $56, and sewing a button was another saving. It was a way of relating to her man. Of making him hers. Of giving herself. Of being useful. Of being a girl.

Of course, it had to pay off. It wasn't for nothing. Being a woman didn't mean not getting fair treatment. But it was value. Value for value.

A body could be of some use, and that was the way you got back reward, love, money. Life wasn't a rip off because you had gone to some school, come from some family, belonged to some class, or even because you were an American.

Life was a labor. A service. A quid pro quo.

Sex was a favor too, even a duty, but you did it for love - indeed, you worked for love. But it wasn't for nothing. At the end of the day you got back love too.

Rosalie's was a kind of economics, in fact; only it didn't have to do with money. It was an exchange. It was barter. You bartered favor for favor, attention for attention, body for body.

You worked, you served, you gave. It was the kind of economics that the lilies of the field understood, not the Alumni, the professionals, the educated. Literacy was counting on your fingers and knowing the score without the accounts, the banks, the brokerages, and the tax men.

A body for a body.

A Door to Knock on

One day I read her a newspaper piece about America having no soul.

Unlike the Afghanis, the Jews, the Africans, the Chinese, the Italians - America, it said, had no soul. That's what it said.

Soulless people live anonymous, mechanical, robot, cybernetic, computer type lives in America - there is no soul. The people have no souls, just bodies. One walks the streets among empty shadows and stuffed men, hollow men.

"It depends," she said, "on which door you knock on."

Six Vega Lane

Six Vega Lane. I loved that house. It was just a tract house, a normal raised ranch, one door garage, three bedrooms, one bath - nothing special about it. A modular space age housing unit developed up on nowhere, Somewhere Lane, USA, but it was hers.

The yellow flowers clustered star-like by the broken front door. She had to mow; she had to shovel; she had to prune. Twigs and branches fell down in the winter. There were patches of dead brown grass in the lawn from the fertilizer. The windows had no curtains. The poof sofas took up all the space in the parlor. One was already threadbare. The glass table with plastic and pink cushions filled the dining cubicle. Outside lay a third of God's acre.

Inside, there were fifty-nine photos and pictures of her family around on the walls and dresser. The flower boxes on the back deck grew just fine. There was a beat-up barbecue. It was not my home. It was her home. Home, and not much else.

Six Vega Lane, like a driveway in a galaxy of everyday stars, a number in a crowded suburban constellation, a corner of nobodies and nowhere in a rented heaven without big names, big people, or big ideas. Somewhere City, USA.

Just somewhere average along the road where she had sewed, cooked, mowed, and shoveled. I loved it because it wasn't myself; because it was hers, and she let me in.

This was where she rattled among the pots, where the burner and shelf space wasn't big enough, where the sink was too small, where the shower curtain didn't fit.

I loved it because I had had nothing to do with it; she simply welcomed me and made me at home in Somewhere City, USA, and it became somewhere else. It was her space, consecrated by life. Her life.

I loved it because there was nothing of mine here, no shadow of me, of my past. I loved it because I would never have picked it, furnished it, or ever even lived there - but I could have, with her, that is; she would have made it home.

I loved it because if it hadn't been for her I might have hated it, but it was a mirror: clean, light, simple, unencumbered. Light wood floors, nothing heavy, nothing sad; just the pots to rattle all packed on top of each other in the scanty cupboard.

It was Rosalie's. A nondescript piece of free, average America, only neater, and cleaner, worth about one hundred thousand dollars, all but the last payment paid for, four hundred and ten dollars - for the money: a few trees, a forsythia, and one squirrel, Charley, who lived there.

It was her patch of earth. That's what made it a piece of real estate for me. And to sell it was like selling our heart. It was that simple.

Like selling a first kiss or some other memory, the place where she had proved to me what she was.

Vega Lane. The name of a star.

Maybe it was corny, but true. An alley somewhere lit by the sun. Simple. Light. Clean. Neat. A tract house.

A window on a not-through street. A road going nowhere.

This was the long end of the beginning.

There may be millions of them. But this was Rosalie's. Even her house plant had grown there for as many years as she had been there.

And the road to nowhere, after all, had led to her house.

The Balcony

The last thing she ever expected to own was a balcony. And this is why: a balcony has a view.

Yes, we stood in the parking lot, among the omnipresent cars, and she said: "I will never leave here until I have a balcony."

The sun was setting. We couldn't see it because of the skyscrapers. We were in Big City.

"It costs four dollars an hour just to stand here," I told her, "do you realize what eternity will cost?"

"I don't care. The house is gone," she said, and besides, the tract house had had no balcony.

Most American houses are built for winter; porches and terraces are for summer, not balconies.

The sun in America usually sets somewhere around the corner, not in plain view. Juliet's balcony scene is an anachronism in the age of TV. There is no longer any place for the forlorn lover to jump from. All the windows are sealed shut and climate controlled.

"We may have been poor," she said, "we may have slept six to a room. It was the war. Papa, he was missing in action on the eastern front - but we had a balcony. I could get out of the apartment and shut myself on the balcony for hours, I remember. Even if it was war. It was my place. Just big enough for a person."

"Well, this is America and we don't have balconies. I'm sorry. We have back yards."

She began to cry. That balcony was long ago and far away and she had been a child. Childhood is a balcony on the world. A balcony is a view on to somewhere, a window above the world, a picture of the sun setting westward where, when one grows up, one will go with time and be in the view that from the balcony you just looked at motionless, outside, above the void.

Yes, we are always moving on, can never go back, not for long. "Life changes," I said, "the balcony is not for ever. Some people work all their lives and never sit on a balcony. You were lucky. You were young. But you can't stand in the parking lot forever just because you don't have a balcony."

She wanted to dance on the balcony. It was as if life were a song, a performance, and she wanted the balcony to dance on, like a stage before the curtain fell, before the last act ended.

"Mussolini had a balcony," I told her. "It's all a fascist dream. In America we have back yards, back yards and trailers, not balconies. I could get you the trailer."

"I will never, ever ever, *ever* live in a trailer," she repeated. She got no solace from this argument and wouldn't budge. "I can cook for you. You could get me a balcony." Oh, I thought, somewhere in Italy, in Spain, in Greece, is a little balcony where she could stand and look into the future and see the palm trees, the desert, the mountains, the city. But not here in a parking lot.

I was wrong.

As I looked up, I saw a row of town houses overlooking the wharf where we stood in the parking lot, and under each roof was, yes, a small balcony!

It was as if I had never seen them before, as if they were waiting for - for what! Her memories? Her childhood? For long ago and far away?

"If you shut your eyes for a moment," I said, "I'll surprise you. Don't move!"

She promised and held her breath there by the car until I got back. I ran. Oh, how I ran! It was like the speed-up sequences in a movie. To the real estate broker, to the bank, to the tax man, to town hall. I mortgaged a whole life and signed up for thirty years of 7.85 per cent and points and payments out of God knows what as if money really could be found in the gutters, like leaves, and it was all done, I had the key, and I came panting back to the parking lot and, yes, she was still there, the girl who had hid on the balcony, where she had her own doll's room, and I said to her, "I've done it."

"What have you done?" she asked dubiously.

"I bought a balcony," I announced.

It was like the story of the young man by the Ganges who went up to the old man sitting by the stone on the roadway, and the young man asked, "What is the meaning of life?"

The old man said, "I'll tell you, but first would you go to that house and get me a drink of water."

The young man went to the house, knocked on the door, and a young girl of the house let him in.

"Could I have a drink of water for the old man?" he asked, and the young girl said yes, and took him to the kitchen, where he found her so pretty he began to talk with her and forgot the old man.

It wasn't until night that he remembered where he was, and the family asked him to sleep over. He slept in the attic.

The next day the girl was as charming as ever and he went out into the field with her father. So it went day after day. Finally, he married the young girl, and they had children. They lived happily until one day, as the children were almost grown, a great flood came and swept their house away, drowning the young man's wife and the children, and the whole family, and after all the years of work and child-raising and joy and sadness, the flood swept the young man himself down the river until he thought he was going to drown too, but he washed up on the side of the river, a grown man himself now, and there was the same old man.

"Oh," said the old man with some surprise, "it's you again. Now I can tell you the meaning of life."

Yes, Rosalie was still there in the parking lot.

"I bought a balcony," I said to her again.

"Where did you get the money?"

Now, whenever the wind changes and I think of us out there in America, I invite her to the balcony, overlooking the cityscape, where we sit on the white plastic chairs dreaming a dream.

The Arch of Triumph

The majestic alleyway led Rosalie and me up lengthwise along the city through the arbors of platan trees to the Arch of Triumph. We were visiting the Capitol.

This urban diamond was the monument of monuments overlooking the urbane surroundings. Cornices and niches housed the triumphs and commemorations of centuries to the heroes and leaders of the nation. The busts and reliefs decorated the stone monolith at the head of the broad avenue. Overhead the blue sky scudded with clouds of remembrance.

City revelers and pedestrians crowded the street and its shops and cafes. The autos skirted crazily around the arch and into the intersecting avenues. Buses drew up and hugged the curbs, emptying sightseers into the rush. Everywhere people took photographs of themselves. A white noise of the populace rose up from the streets.

A city targets its memories. Inscriptions on the arch recorded all the national battles and campaigns of the centuries. Regimental and army insignias decorated the stone. Flags flew from the pinnacles and the sidewalk itself was inscribed with memories of wars, victories, and battles. An invisible honor guard of the nation stood by guarding the memories of a people, and along the long avenue the echo of footsteps and boots seemed to muffle into the day to day buzz of the city.

It was here, like a song, I came to know Rosalie's inner self. Vendors selling flowers at the corners and curbs dotted the crosswalk that went under the road out to the arch and surfaced under the giant, towering structure.

The cosmopolitan view, like a national memory, etched down the long avenue, and the populace seemed to crowd around itself thriving on its sense of centrality.

Rosalie herself was quiet. We held hands surreptitiously under the arch.

The uniformed guards stood on grim duty.

Then she began to sob.

At first I thought she was realizing something sad about us, maybe that we were not right for each other, that we should part, or that death would, after all, separate us. We would not be buried in an urn together. We would not be mingled for eternity.

But it was not that.

Her sobbing was uncontrollable. She shook on the pavement.

It was as if she had suddenly lost everything.

I couldn't understand. The weather was perfect. The blue sky and rainless air warmed and comforted us. The cafes were bright with bustle. We had some money in our pockets. We were in love. We were dancing in the street.

But she shook like an orphan in the wind. I looked down.

At our feet was the tomb of the unknown soldier: a man missing, a man dead, a man who died nameless for the future. I remembered.

At last, it was her father she was crying for. He had never come back from the Eastern Front when she was a child of four years old. Missing in action. The hardest fate for the widow. A little girl, too, facing the future half orphan, without a father.

I remembered too her mother. The small woman who had gone out to clean house and do laundry to support four children. The two-room tenement still stood where she had grown up after the war, the narrow balcony view over the fatherless street. The empty lot opposite, where the military cars parked. An empty lot like the grave of a father.

Somehow all the years, like the lost memory of an ancient war, had been empty until this moment for her, when at the forlorn tomb of the unknown soldier she found the man who had been missing all her life.

Now I was that man.

I was raised by her love from the battle of life and took the shoes of a man who had left in uniform so many decades before and never come back. I meant to her the fulfillment that he had never been able to give. I was like a soldier, a refugee returned.

I meant more to her than just myself, a whole memory, a promise in her life filled.

There, under the Arch of Triumph, she clutched for a moment her empty memory just as she held on to my arm and shook with the emotion of decades. It was like standing with a doll on the balcony.

So, after all, the battles and defeats and victories of a nation were not just empty ciphers of armies, but the longings and fate of people we knew, and never knew. The headlines of time rode on the nameless name of a young person like her father. Bravery was fulfilled. Promise restored. Flesh and blood renewed. All this in a second on the upward glance of a shining, lonely girl.

History itself seemed to collect in her tears. Flowers

on the sidewalk, bouquets on a tomb, reminded us all of dreams and the glory of girlhood.

I took her back in my arms, dumb at not having sensed her loss, at not knowing I was the one who had returned from the battle of life to fulfill her dream, but that she was ready for me because she had lost a father; and she was making up for his life, his loss, his death.

Yes, she was ironing shirts; yes, she was cooking those missing meals.

Life tries to make up for itself and overcome its past. I was a link in the chain of love stretching past into the shadows of mankind and of nations. This was the meaning of a tomb. This was the meaning of her sobs.

We clung to each other as if bombs were bursting in midair and the rockets were lighting the night.

War is the constant ravage against which only love and regeneration prevails. We were a living pedestrian statue atop the tomb, attesting to the power of survival.

She, I thought, should be the figure atop the arch, Rosalie, a kind of liberty girl with a torch, witness to the trial of time and all the rest of mankind's tender moments.

Deafly, I seemed to hear the marches, the bands, the music of history at our feet, a parade of peoples, a review of history at our back, and unwittingly I knew at last that she would cling to me and I to her in defiance of old age and time, and in the firm knowledge that we too were the fabric of a love story that would only fade at the sunset of eternity's movie.

But that, even then, in fact we would continue to dance on the pavement and in the urn, mingled like ashes, like unknown soldiers in the tomb.

A Cool Million

Yet with a new sadness, I took Rosalie back up to the Hideaway where we had first had a Greek supper together and danced the evening away to oldies by a live singer and keyboard man. The dance floor was small and crowded by tables but it was our crowd, elder dates in throes of urban romance neatly dressed and holding each other close.

The Hideaway was where I first impulsively said to Rosalie that we should be buried together, should mix our ashes in the urn. It seemed so simple. So final now.

Rosalie had no idea of what was up when we returned to the table, and she was radiant. That pixie smile of contentment crowned her face. It looked as if she were gazing off into some happy distance.

We sat at the same table where we had talked of the urn, the one we were supposed to buy in Palermo - only death had become much more real.

"You look so serious," she said. "That's not a dance face."

I mugged a smile. What could Rosalie know?

I hadn't the heart either to break it to her. When I say heart, too, I speak advisedly - because that was what I had: a broken heart. Not the romantic kind. But the kind in real time, in total virtuality. A heart that had simply lived and loved too much. A heart burdened with its own age. A worn-out heart.

"Rosalie," I said.

"Whatly?" She was all eager, as if this were our night.

"Rosalie. I've made my will."

"Your will?" She looked nonplussed. Then she scratched the table cloth with the fork. "Am I in it?"

"Yes," I murmured. A pregnant silence fell between us. "Rosalie. I have less than a year to live. Maybe weeks. Maybe days."

"Days?"

"The doctor says I'm a walking epitaph. He says to wrap up my affairs immediately. He says I can expect to drop any minute."

"Any minute?" Rosalie said, with parted lips. "You're joking! How can a doctor know when you're going to die?"

"It's a new procedure," I smiled. "An advance in prognosis. They have a new machine that tells you when you die. It's part of cyberspace. The medical profession, at last, sees into the future now." I hiccuped. "It's all over, Rosalie. I'm sorry."

"It was just beginning," she said.

I shrugged.

"You get a million, Rosalie. You can live happily ever after."

I thought she would get angry, start to shout at me.

"It's not my fault, Rosalie." I reached for her hand.

"What about us?" she asked. "Didn't you think about us?"

"That's all I think of. But not the new machine. You stand on it, and it tells you when you're going to die. Simple."

"Like scales?" she said.

She looked at me as if I had told a joke that she didn't understand.

"Sorry," I said. "You lose."

When I am an Angel

When I die, my agenda from the other world is to do something for Rosalie. As soon as I get there I will be thinking of her. It is not clear what one can do from the other world, from the spiritual world, for a person here, in this world, but whatever it is I will do it for Rosalie.

They say that only the living can do something for the dead. This is because the living still have eyes and ears and hands and feet. When you're still alive you can pray for a dead person - you can even see, hear and think for them.

I certainly hope Rosalie will do this for me. Rosalie had never thought about this but if she knew there were still something to do for me, she would be busy. Why shouldn't I do what I can for her when I am dead?

I will be in another modality, of course, but perhaps I can influence her mood, her thoughts, her luck. Perhaps I can influence her fate. This is the kind of thing that one may be involved in when one is dead. Maybe death is a kind of lottery. I can send her thoughts, or, more likely, feelings. I could help her not to be alone.

Maybe the dead are with us. Maybe they live inside us.

She will probably not still be a waitress, of course, or maybe she will go back to waitressing when I am gone. I could look after her heartbeat from the world of beyond.

Maybe that's the kind of thing the dead do for us. I could help her not to trip going down the steps.

I could just be with her.

They say the truth is not complete without the dead; they say when you are alive you shouldn't forget the dead - although you shouldn't forget the living either. But they say nothing about what the dead are supposed to do for the living.

But I know.

I can be close to her when she is sleeping.

I can be a thought in her mind.

The Doctor's Machine

I was going to die, so what would become of Rosalie? How would she dance without me? A million dollars would get her through - feed the body at least - but what about the soul? Her soul would be alone, unless I could communicate with her from Heaven - or Hell.

It seemed to me that when I was gone I could shine down on her, although certainly I wouldn't be able to talk. After-death is the least explored place by science, after all, and I wasn't much interested in what religion had to say about me and Rosalie and the afterlife. It was all so sentimental and so moral. What interested me was what I could do for Rosalie, or Rosalie could do for me. She could pray, of course. But I wouldn't be able to speak. Only to think, when you're dead, would be lucky. Maybe I would have wings, but thought is wings. I wanted in space, or wherever the afterlife is, to be able to think of Rosalie, because I knew that would help her. Thinking of a person always helps them.

I would be out there travelling through the planets to the fixed stars, on into the primum mobile, into the ether, and I would be shedding my body, my feelings, my life.

They say you see it all backwards and that it takes a third of your real life to get back through your own biography. In that case, I would be busy. Would I be on a star?

All I knew was that from the afterlife I wanted to send

Rosalie some kind of a message, some kind of a bouquet. It would be only my intentions probably that she could receive, only my inspirations.

Perhaps from the other world I could see through her eyes! That would be something. When I left earth she would be all the eyes and ears that were left to me. My own would be cremated. Perhaps her sensations and perceptions would float up to me in that ethereal afterlife space and from them I could be with her, or send her back a thought. Perhaps the dead can influence brains and minds from far away and have a way, the way of intuitions, of speaking to the living. That was what I hoped for Rosalie.

I wanted to help her guardian angel for her after I died, although I supposed that was wishing too much; it would be enough if I could send her light, joy, love.

If she woke in the morning, and had the thought: I am thinking of you - that would be me.

Maybe the afterlife is measured among the living. Their prayers would, to the dead, be as a kind of manna, a food, flowers that have been spiritualized and have wings. The wings of movement. The wings of intention.

I said to Rosalie: "Our abstractions - truth, beauty, goodness - may be real in the true outer-space of after-death, just the way a flower here may be the thought of an angel, the touch of a star." This was after the doctor's machine had doomed me.

Maybe love in the language of afterlife is a beautiful landscape, or something as beautiful as a landscape. The afterlife may be all a translation into another realm, another language.

And maybe from there, there would be a language for reaching Rosalie, a modality that changed eternity into the everyday thoughts and feelings of her heart.

No matter what the doctor's machine said, I would be there. But would Rosalie know it was me? Sure. Who else could it be? She would know because love is a kind of knowledge that translates the world of forever into the world of now.

Rosalie would miss me, of course. It would be a kind of absence, a void. But a void is the beginning of the invisible. Yes. At last I would be invisible, and Rosalie would no longer be able to judge me on appearances.

And wherever somewhere else is, Rosalie would be there with me. It would be like being in the urn. We fade into a symbol and come out on the other side. Death is an abstraction too. We pierce it like stardust. I would be the missing-ness that she would feel where once I had been, and maybe eternity is like that. An ache.

Only, I know, that down there, up there, out there, I would miss not being able to step up to her and take her in my arms and dance, as we used to, or, with all those angels, sing her a song. Yes, death is probably the inability to do what you want to do. In eternity the soul is busy doing other things.

All these thoughts came to me the night after we sat in the Hideaway, and I told Rosalie that the doctor's machine had predicted death.

In the morning I woke up.

I was still here, waiting. Aren't we all? But I turned on my side, without waking her, and studied that tidy little face, the small nostrils, the turned down nose, the tight mouth, the shut eyes of the waitress.

All those trays she had carried seemed far away. All the meals she had served.

Rosalie, Rosalie.

Yes, she was breathing.

Death Turns Out to be True

The doctor's machine was right. I was dead within a few weeks. It half crazed Rosalie.

Mark Twain had it right. Death isn't half so difficult as it looks; everybody does it.

As Mickey Spillane said, "It was easy."

What happens in the end is you just slip away, like a giant snail in deep water. Your body is like a shell; it floats up on the beach; you leave it behind, like something on the sand washed up after the fact.

The fact of death itself is a little unpleasant; I mean, I wouldn't want to do it again - what happens, in fact, is that the body sort of gets rid of you. It's like birth.

It's a little violent in that sense, but then so is love. It's painful, but so is life.

They say the light at the end is beautiful, and I guess that's so. What I found comforting, however, was the darkness. It was deep, thick, and soft, like down, or like a giant comforter.

Rosalie was there, too.

In fact, I didn't feel that I ever really left her, she was so much a part of me by this time. Death, if anything, is like a delusion. You aren't aware anymore, in a certain sense, of what is happening, and, like a dream, you think something else is going on.

I mean, for instance, that I felt I was going somewhere with Rosalie.

The future seemed like a trip and we would be together somewhere else, but when you're dying you don't exactly pack the bags and know where you're going. It just happens.

I wasn't even exactly conscious that I was dying, because when you do this your mind is already somewhere else. The body is no longer important, and I may have been even sort of asleep when I did it.

The body was important to Rosalie, however.

There it was.

My corpse.

In the bed.

I guess you could say that was still me, although, since I am a story teller, and a fabulist to boot, I am really telling this all before it happened, because, I know, when I die, I can no longer type. The body is an instrument, after all. Not even a computer works when the electricity is gone. And when you're dead you no longer have the instrument, any more than you have the electricity or can hold a pen.

Rosalie simply looked at me.

She said, "He's dead."

She got an awful wrench though. Something in her heart broke too, just like a twig snapping, and she knew I was gone. I was awfully sorry for her. I remember that, although I had other things on my mind. She was left with the mess.

Every good story has to have a body, a corpse, and usually a gun. In this case there was no gun. No smoking clue to the murderer. No fingerprints. It was the perfect crime. A whodunit in which I was the victim of my own mystery. Unless you want to blame death on God. Who else could have done it? Who else was there? Rosalie?

Is every woman the death of her man, and vice versa?

Rosalie didn't know what to do so she pulled the sheet up over my face, but not before giving me a little kiss.

It was a chaste kiss. It felt soft and cool, as always, needy almost; Rosalie's had always been needy kisses. She had always kissed as if she had never quite gotten enough to eat. I had never really satisfied her, in fact, not even when I was alive.

Rosalie needed more than life could give, in a way, but I know I was sorry I couldn't kiss her back. Life isn't fair, I know, but neither is death. After she kissed me, she folded the sheet up over my eyes and it was like a veil; I couldn't see her clearly anymore. Then she called the doctor.

I don't know why everyone calls the doctor at this time. The machine had already told him I was going to die, and besides there wasn't anything more that he could do now that I was dead.

Rosalie, up till now, had been a normal girl. She had her training as a waitress. When the customers are done, you collect the tip, clear the table and wipe up. You get rid of the dirty dishes.

Then you cash out.

The Wedding

The wedding took place after the funeral. It was Rosalie's idea - but, I admit, I inspired her from the world of the angels. I had been cremated, of course, so I was already in the urn that Rosalie and I had picked out. It was the one we had seen in Palermo.

In those last days, we had gone back to get it, the terracotta vase outside the store on the Conca d'Oro up above Palermo in the sun, the one that had been used as an ashtray. It was our last trip.

We took it after the doctor's machine told me I would be dead in a few weeks, and I don't remember much, except that I talked a lot, and we stayed in an awfully good hotel, sparing no expense, and we ate an awful lot of ice cream. Italian *gelato*. We even went dancing.

The Italians don't have much ballroom dancing anymore, but we went to a Sicilian disco and held each other closely in a crowd of young people and waltzed slightly back and forth to the punk rock and the rest of the music that they imported from America.

Rosalie kept saying, "I love to dance."

But I was telling about the wedding.

Rosalie decided to get married after I died, after reading the will.

As I have tried to show, Rosalie was in some ways a

simple girl, and she couldn't bear not being married if she was to get all that money.

The estate, after all, was hers. She was the remainder woman. But she wanted to be a regular widow. Rosalie had a sense of propriety. She had a sense of common decency. Now that she was rich she didn't need to be a waitress anymore, but she wanted to be a widow. A proper widow.

She also was worried that she herself might die. Already she felt mortal. But she thought, if she died, and we were mixed as ashes in the urn - as my will stipulated - we would be living in sin, or at least dead together in sin, and she wanted to make sure. Rosalie always had to have it right.

When I was still living, I had joked to her that in order to get married we would need a Papal dispensation and that we could get one for about $50,000 from the Sacred Rotary.

Rosalie took me seriously now that I was dead, and she thought she needed a Papal dispensation to marry a dead man, even though we were not Catholics. She may be right.

She went to St. Leonard's Peace Garden to ask the priest about it, and he said, "What do you want to marry a dead man for?"

They had never had this problem before in his diocese. Well, every woman has her reasons.

Rosalie began to cry and said, "I just want a normal husband."

The priest patted her on the head. Rosalie wasn't the first woman he had met who wanted a normal man, but even so, he thought she was overcome by grief.

"Whatever you do," he said thoughtfully, "don't marry a memory. My daughter, what is it you do?"

"I'm a waitress."

This stumped him. He couldn't think of anything further to say, and he gave Rosalie a blessing.

So, without a Papal dispensation, she got married in Vermont. In Vermont, you don't even need a blood test.

Nor is there a law against marrying a dead man, and even the Justice of the Peace can do it.

But Rosalie wanted to get married in church. She had never had a church wedding and besides she had already, when I was still alive, bought the dress. It was an off-white dirndl, with a dipping neckline, short hem, and embroidered bust. She had even bought it on my credit card and signed my name.

Rosalie made all the arrangements. After all, her mother and father were both dead. She was an orphan. An orphan marrying a dead man. She sent out little engraved invitations and, with my money, invited everyone at her expense to stay the night in the local inn. It was a November day. Light snow had premeditated the season and the village was covered in a few inches of fine powder. The world was white, as if it had put on Rosalie's bridal gown.

Already by four o'clock it was getting dark and the white church loomed up with yellow lights, like candles, in the windows under the almost gray sky. Guests, her friends, my family, walked up the snowy street to the white door with the white ribbon hanging in front.

She had ordered herself a yellow bouquet. Even my brother was there in a dark suit, and he read the lesson from St. John - no, from Corinthians - about love clashing like a clanging cymbal.

Rosalie was five minutes late.

In church, all the people sat silently waiting in the pews, and I couldn't believe, that if I had been alive, anybody at all would have bothered to come to our wedding. But it was a thrilling kind of pleasure to see them all, to think that Rosalie and I were worth all this trouble.

135

As she came up the steps of the church in the early dark in her white dirndl, smiling an ecstatic little smile, Rosalie was again and forever beautiful.

It was as if life was making up to her all the dinners she had ever waited on, all the service she had ever given, all the patience and givingness she had ever had. It was if God were making it up to her in this moment for the death of her father.

She even remembered the war, when they went down to the barracks to see him off, and she had climbed up on to his bunk, gone to sleep, and wet his bed.

Now, at last, she was a bride.

She carried our urn on a tray like a true waitress into the church, and the great organ struck up the Volunteer's March. All the heads turned.

There was Rosalie, her arm around the urn. She did it with dignity, I must say. From her face you would have scarcely known that I was a dead man.

She had invited my cousin to co-celebrate the service, and she stood there facing the altar with the urn at her side, the golden candlesticks, the golden cross, and the American flag. The numbers of the hymns from the regular service were stricken from the black plaque and instead, for the vows, the Ave Maria was sung.

The Ave Maria wafted up soft and mysterious into the white rafters of the church blessing this invisible union of life and death, of Rosalie and me, and the words mingled with the dust of time past, time present, and time future like a poem of the sea and the morning star over the blue choppy waters of eternity.

Rosalie sat beside the urn and solemnly said, "I do."

Nobody will believe this, but when the priest turned

to the urn and asked if I would, for better or worse, take Rosalie to be my wedded wife and share all my worldly goods with her, there was a rustle from inside the ashes, and they said, "I do."

Nobody since the Medieval Ages has seen a girl kiss death, but that's what Rosalie did, and when he was finished the priest said, "I pronounce you man and wife."

There was a flash. Somebody had taken an illegal photograph inside the church.

They used to say photographs from the other side of the moon would never come out, but this seemed like a wedding from the other side of the moon. As Rosalie carried the urn out of the church, they sang *Moonlight in Vermont*.

Rosalie, with the urn, greeted everybody one by one coming out of the church, but all I remember is one old man on two canes, about ninety-three, who gave Rosalie a shaky hand and said, "May you live happily together ever after." He was my father. I could still recognize him.

My mother was there too, the dear woman, and she said to Rosalie, "You have a handsome man, dear. God bless. You've done him a world of good."

I have to forgive them for everything. After all, it's not easy to say the right thing at a wedding, especially or even when the groom is living.

Dead, or alive?

Rosalie had brought her man home. It was no mean feat; and I didn't want to ruin her evening.

She put the urn in the car and went to the reception. She wasn't going to dance with an urn. She had her principles. Some people say that life is the dance of death and there were once a lot of pictures around showing the skeletons dancing together. But Rosalie didn't believe in that.

There was music, though. Rosalie had hired a three piece band, bass, flute, and guitar, and our friend, the accordion man, had shown up too.

It should have been our last dance. Whatever, Rosalie, at least, danced all night. If you could see her as I do you know she was just perfect for the movie.

No, Rosalie was no doctor, lawyer, baker, or candlestick maker, she was not a seamstress, clerk, salesgirl, buyer, or one of those new lady executives that chair our computer world - she was a waitress, plain and simple. She carried dishes and slung pizza. She had done it for years. I had always dreamed of loving a waitress.

They move so well.

They don't hang around waiting for the end of the world. Always on the move, they scurry back and forth, are always on their feet, and don't have to do fitness exercises. They can count. And they can remember. They have heads for orders. Service is the name of their trade.

She was like that too: no slouch. Not someone always complaining of a headache. Every day she took her shower, prettied up, and put on her little black trousers and white top, with a necktie, and hurried off to work. Now, she was even a bride.

The Last Day

Rosalie punched in at the time clock just after 3.45 - 3.46, to be exact. It was her last day. Then she checked the computer. She was number three. Her lucky number. "So this is your last day," Maria, the owner's mother said. "And I haven't even met your husband."

"Nope," Rosalie said.

Maria was looking for an invitation. All she wants, Rosalie thought, is to check out the furniture, see how much the house cost, what she had for a man. Ha! Ha!

Maria just wanted to gossip. All she needed was to find out about the urn. She had heard that Rosalie got married - but had not even sent a card.

Rosalie pulled six tables on her station, four on the mezzanine, and a two and a six downstairs. They turned over three times; she had eighteen parties. There was one tip of $35 on the six, and several tens on thirty dollar chits. None of the restaurant regulars showed up. It was a Friday.

The years, the trays, the money was what Rosalie thought of. She had no grand thoughts, no great memories. It was her life. It was her work.

The owner came over.

"So this is it," he said. "It's been a long time." He looked vaguely at the wall. She was his best number, his best waitress; she had only called in once in all those years.

Rosalie, in black pants, black socks, black low shoes, with my own best yellow necktie on. All that food - where had it gone?

The hard earned dollars that every night she counted at the kitchen table against the bills. From hand to mouth it had been, with not a penny left over, and the years gone like sand. It was all numbers. Number three on the computer, her number, then the number of the table, the number of guests, the number of their time in, the number of the dish, of the drinks, and finally the final number: the price. There were four cooks.

She picked her order up by number in the kitchen. When she cashed out, it was a number.

Service produces no product; it vanished like time, like a smile, like the last cup of coffee. Rosalie felt almost nothing.

Gino's even seemed a little strange to her, as if she were a new girl. There was not even a last snapshot.

The owner had nothing more to say. He never had done much for the girls. They had formed the Freedom Club - $10 a month dues, visits, drinks after work, sometimes a dinner, sometimes an outing. Freedom from Gino's!

Rosalie's mouth didn't even water tonight for the veal parm. She wasn't hungry.

The last girl who had left got a gold watch. Rosalie might wait for one, but she wasn't counting on it. Gold was the right color for Rosalie, though, for all those years; but all the owner said was: "So, give me your address." But it was half-hearted. The customers loved Rosalie, but all the owner loved was money.

The girls were just money and time to him, except that Rosalie had always brought more into the cash register than the rest.

Then the owner said, "Well, I'm going to retire number three."

He said, "Yes, I'm going to retire your apron."

She did her sidework, took out the dirties, did some napkins, some salt and peppers, washed the tables, sniffed slightly, and got ready to shut down early.

A girl's life is like a pink seashell. Time washes it up on the shore, and inside nothing is left but the sound of the sea. And the muscle. She still had all that muscle from the trays.

Life was a workout. She was married now - to an urn, to a dead man. She had gone to the altar. But inside she was clean - work cleans you out.

Service doesn't leave anything but the signs. The signs and the disposition. A waitress runs up credit in the other world. She comes away with an IOU in her favor, a credit. No glamour photo of her as one of the hundred greatest stars of all time. Not much in the way of memories either. Just a gut feeling. A feeling of having done it.

She cashed out. One hundred and seventeen dollars. It was the last time.

"So shall we go?" the girls said.

A last drink.

Even the cooks came. The cooks had never ever come to a farewell drink for one of the girls, but Rosalie was special. It was nothing she said - it was her being.

"You don't want wine," the cook told her at the bar, "you want something special."

Tonight would never come again.

A Kahlua stinger. She had two. The Freedom Club paid.

You can count the dollars. You can count the time.

Tomorrow she would never come back. There must be something to say.

Some final word. A cadenza.

But all that happened was the girls hugging her at the door and waving as she walked away from it.

"We love you," they said.

It was over. Maria had not even said goodbye. The owner, he was retiring the apron.

But Rosalie walked away numb from it for the last time.

"I don't need them," Rosalie said to herself.

"If I had thought it was my last day, I think I would have had a heart attack. I was really sort of out of it. In a dither. I wasn't really going to ask for something good to eat, a last meal, although I guess my boss would have given it to me. But I certainly wasn't going to ask."

When you're done, after all, you cash out.